PUFFIN CANADA

SHELL SHOCKED

ERIC WALTERS is the highly acclaimed, bestselling author of over sixty novels for children and young adults. His novels have won the Silver Birch and Red Maple Awards, as well as numerous other prizes, including the White Pine, Snow Willow, Tiny Torgi, Ruth Schwartz, the IODE Violet Downey, and the National Outdoor Book Awards. He has received honours from the Canadian Library Association Book Awards and the Children's Book Centre, and is a recipient of UNESCO's international award for Literature in Service of Tolerance.

To find out more about Eric and his novels, or to arrange for him to speak at your school, visit his website at www.ericwalters.net.

Also by Eric Walters from Penguin Canada

CAMP X
SHELL SHOCKED

ERIC WALTERS

PUFFIN
CANADA

PUFFIN CANADA

Published by the Penguin Group

Penguin Group (Canada), 90 Eglinton Avenue East, Suite 700, Toronto, Ontario, Canada M4P 2Y3
    (a division of Pearson Canada Inc.)

Penguin Group (USA) Inc., 375 Hudson Street, New York, New York 10014, U.S.A.
Penguin Books Ltd, 80 Strand, London WC2R 0RL, England
Penguin Ireland, 25 St Stephen's Green, Dublin 2, Ireland (a division of Penguin Books Ltd)
Penguin Group (Australia), 250 Camberwell Road, Camberwell, Victoria 3124, Australia
    (a division of Pearson Australia Group Pty Ltd)
Penguin Books India Pvt Ltd, 11 Community Centre, Panchsheel Park, New Delhi – 110 017, India
Penguin Group (NZ), 67 Apollo Drive, Rosedale, Auckland 0632, New Zealand
    (a division of Pearson New Zealand Ltd)
Penguin Books (South Africa) (Pty) Ltd, 24 Sturdee Avenue, Rosebank, Johannesburg 2196, South Africa

Penguin Books Ltd, Registered Offices: 80 Strand, London WC2R 0RL, England

First published in Puffin Canada paperback by Penguin Group (Canada),
    a division of Pearson Canada Inc., 2010
Published in this edition, 2011

1 2 3 4 5 6 7 8 9 10 (OPM)

LIBRARY AND ARCHIVES CANADA CATALOGUING IN PUBLICATION

Walters, Eric, 1957–
    Shell shocked / Eric Walters.

(Camp X)
ISBN 978-0-14-316789-1

1. World War, 1939–1945—Secret service—Canada—Juvenile fiction. I. Title. II.
    Series: Walters, Eric, 1957– . Camp.

PS8595.A598S54 2011a   jC813'.54   C2011-903121-3

Visit the Penguin Group (Canada) website at **www.penguin.ca**

Special and corporate bulk purchase rates available; please see
www.penguin.ca/corporatesales or call 1-800-810-3104, ext. 2477 or 2474

SHELL SHOCKED

CHAPTER ONE

"WHERE DOES this one go?" I asked.

My mother peeled back one of the flaps on the top of the box and peeked inside. "Put it in the kitchen, George."

"Kitchen it is."

"Many more to bring in?" she asked.

"Not many."

"That's good," my brother Jack said as he came into the room carrying yet another box. "Because I don't think this place can hold much more."

"He's right," I agreed. "This house isn't very big."

"It's a lot smaller than our place in Bowmanville," Jack said.

"Yeah, it's about the same size as the house we lived in in Whitby," I added.

"Well, that's not surprising, because this house and the one in Whitby were both manufactured by the Wartime Housing Corporation," my mother told us.

"They do look pretty much the same," I said.

"All the houses around here look the same," Jack added. "Everything they build looks the same."

"There's no choice," my mother said. "There are lots and lots of people moving here to Ajax to work at the munitions factory, and they all need someplace to live, so they have to build them fast."

"And small."

"Small is relative," she pointed out.

"It's even more *relative* when you have to share a bedroom with your brother," Jack said, and he shot me a dirty look.

"It's not my idea of a picnic either," I said. "But at least I don't snore."

"At least I don't keep my room like a pigsty or——"

"Hey, hey, hey!" Bill yelled out as he entered the room carrying yet another box. "A little peace and quiet, please ... don't make me shoot anybody."

My mother gave him a dirty look.

"I was just kidding around," he said, apologetically.

"That isn't something that should be kidded about," she scolded him, like he was a child.

"Sorry."

Of course Bill would never have shot any of us, but he could have if he'd wanted to. Not only did I know he was carrying a revolver—I'd seen its shape under his jacket—

I knew that he always *had* to carry a weapon. As an officer at Camp X, he wasn't allowed to be without one.

What a bizarre thought. The man helping us move into our new house wasn't just a kind neighbour, he was a spy, a secret agent, a man who was able to go out and kill people … I knew that, because I'd seen him do it.

Bill set his box down on the kitchen counter. "I'm hoping this is going to be your last move for a while," he said.

"*You're* hoping?" I questioned.

"We're *all* hoping," my mother agreed.

"It has been quite the journey," Bill said.

"It makes my head spin." My mother sat down on a kitchen chair, as though she really were dizzy.

"Three moves in less than six months," Jack muttered.

"I still wish we could have stayed at the farm," I said.

"You know that wasn't possible," my mother pointed out. "With your father off fighting in Africa, we couldn't work the farm. Not by ourselves."

My father had enlisted in the army and was with the St. Patrick's Regiment, fighting—and *beating*—the Nazis, chasing them across northern Africa. We had leased our fields to neighbouring farmers to work until we could move back.

"That's why we had to go to Whitby to begin with, so I could work at the munitions factory," my mother said.

"And I imagine that's where you would have stayed, if a couple of young lads hadn't let their curiosity get the better of them," Bill said.

"Sorry," I said.

"Can you blame us?" Jack asked. "What boys wouldn't want to discover what was behind the fence of a secret spy facility like Camp X? Of course we were curious."

"There's an old saying that curiosity killed the cat," my mother noted. "And it almost got you two killed, as well."

"But it *didn't*, and what we did in the end was for the government and the war effort," Jack said. "We were like heroes."

"Almost dead heroes." She turned to Bill. "Would I have even known what had happened to them … how they'd died … if they had died?"

Bill didn't answer right away. Then he slowly shook his head. "I'm not sure if the Official Secrets Act would have allowed us to inform you. It's more likely you would have been told a comforting lie rather than an unpleasant truth."

"I wish I'd known what they were up to," she said. "If I'd known, I might have been able to put an end to this before it got started. Maybe then we wouldn't have had to move to Bowmanville. I still wonder, did we really need to make that move?"

"I'm afraid there was no choice," Bill said. "Those Nazi agents your sons ran up against were neutralized, but there were others, and they knew about the boys. We had to move you to assure that you were safe."

My mother laughed. "That assurance didn't turn out to be worth much."

"In fairness, your safety was guaranteed ... until your boys, again, got too nosy."

"Sorry," I said for a second time. How many times now had I apologized for our adventures?

"So you got Mom a new job," Jack said, "and she ended up working with six hundred and fifty German war prisoners. Was that part of the master plan?"

After we'd left Whitby, our mother had been given a job as a secretary at a prisoner-of-war camp in Bowmanville—a place where they held some of the highest-ranking Germans captured in the war.

"Our employment connections are somewhat limited. Besides, we wanted to be able to keep an eye on you, just in case."

"In case of what?" my mother asked.

"In case the enemy was able to locate you again. Of course, it scarcely crossed our minds that Jack and George would actually go out of their way to find trouble by themselves. We foolishly thought that your boys would go back to being boys ... going to school, delivering papers, playing with their friends. We had no idea that they'd manage to get themselves inside the prisoner-of-war camp."

"It just sort of happened," I said. "But then we were only doing what we were asked to do. We didn't know we'd get involved in an escape attempt."

Bill shook his head. "Let's try something new this time. How about if you *don't* go looking for trouble from now on? Go to school, get a part-time job, find a girlfriend."

"Ugh! We don't want girlfriends!" I said.

Apparently, Jack had other ideas. "Speak for yourself," he said.

"You can both forget about all that," my mother interrupted. "School is your number-one priority. It's hard to come into a new school partway through the year. You'll have to make an effort."

"It's still early in the year," Bill said. "Besides, there are so many new people coming all the time that it isn't like a couple of new students is anything unusual."

"Well, at least I won't have to be the new kid at work," my mother said.

Jack and I exchanged a look. Neither of us was that thrilled that she'd be working again at the DIL complex— that stood for Defence Industries Limited—a factory where they made bombs and shells and explosives. It supplied the ammunition that our troops needed to defeat the Nazis.

"And this time we're living in Ajax instead of Whitby, so I won't be spending so much time getting to work and back. We're so close to the factory that I can walk. That means I can be here to wake you up in the morning, and to make meals and—"

"And to keep an eye on us," Jack said.

She smiled. "That too."

"Keeping an eye on these two wouldn't be the worst idea," Bill agreed.

"You'll be keeping an eye on us anyway, won't you?" I asked Bill.

He smiled slightly but didn't answer—which, of course, was an answer.

"Camp X isn't far away," I said.

"We're right there if you ever need us," Bill said.

"Do you think that … that … you'll ever need *us* again?" I asked.

His smile broadened. "There's no way of telling whether you might be called upon again to—"

"Yes, there is," my mother said. "Boys, your career as spies is over." She turned directly to Bill. "Right?"

He bowed slightly from the waist. "As you wish, madam."

"We came here for a fresh start—we don't want to have to move again," my mother said.

"Oh, that reminds me," Bill said. "There are a few things I need to tell all of you about your fresh start. Perhaps you three should sit down."

I felt a little chill go up my spine. Being asked to sit down was never a good thing.

CHAPTER TWO

"GEORGE."

I started out of my thoughts—or rather lack of thoughts—and looked up at my teacher. "Yes, ma'am?"

"You need to go down to the office to see Mr. McGregor."

There was a chorus of *ooohs* from the other kids at the mention of the principal.

"Did he say why?" I asked.

She scowled. "Go," she said, and pointed to the door.

Slowly I got up. Every eye was on me. This couldn't be good. But then again, how bad could it be? I couldn't think of anything I'd done that might possibly have landed me in trouble … except for maybe falling asleep at my desk a couple of times … that had to be it.

Then I remembered that I'd been late this morning. It wasn't really my fault. My watch had stopped. It was an old watch that had belonged to my grandfather, and my father had once mentioned to me that he'd worn it when he was a kid. I'd found it in the bottom of one of the boxes when we were moving this time. Jack gave me a hard time about using it. He said, "If you can't depend on a watch all the time, you can't depend on it any of the time." I just liked wearing it. It was a little piece of my father when he was so far away.

The hall was empty and I could hear my footsteps echo in the silence. I started to get anxious inside and then stopped myself. I'd faced men with guns. I'd stared straight into the face of Nazi agents threatening to kill me. What was the worst this man could do? Yell at me? Well ... he did have a strap, and I'd heard that he wasn't afraid to use it. And he did always seem to be out in the schoolyard at recess watching people ... in fact, a couple of times I'd thought he was watching *me*. I started to feel anxious again.

I stopped in front of the office and took a couple of deep breaths. I wanted to be calm, look calm, act calm, like I'd done nothing wrong. I opened the door ... and saw Jack sitting there.

"Jack, what did you do?"

"I guess I could ask you the same thing." He looked over at the secretary. "Any idea?"

She barely looked up from her typewriter, shook her head slightly and kept typing, hardly missing a keystroke.

At that same instant the door to the principal's office opened and Mr. McGregor appeared. He was older—sort of a grandfather age—and he had grey hair and matching bushy moustache and eyebrows. He stood straight, like a soldier, and he was large, well built through the shoulders. In his time he would have been a pretty formidable man. I guessed he still was. He smiled—that was good—and motioned us to come in.

"Please, sit," he said, gesturing to two chairs.

We sat down, and he circled around and took a seat behind his desk. He picked up a file folder from the papers scattered there and began to read while we sat waiting—*anxiously* waiting. Finally he looked up from the file.

"I always make it a point to sit down with each new student," he said.

"That must keep you pretty busy," Jack said.

"Yes, John, the student population here has certainly been growing lately."

I almost reacted to Jack being called John, but I didn't. Part of our "fresh start" involved disguising who we really were. We had to somehow not be traceable if somebody—especially Nazi agents—came looking for us. "Jack" was kind of a less formal version of the name "John," and John was my brother's real name, according to his birth certificate and all the school records. We thought going by "John" would be one really easy way to hide a bit. But my brother wasn't happy about going along with the game.

"Actually, most of the time I get called Jack," he said.

"And what does your teacher call you?" Mr. McGregor asked.

"She calls me John, but my friends call me Jack."

"Well, since I'm your principal and not a friend, I think I will call you John. And I strongly suggest that you have everybody call you by your given name. You are not a child any more."

"Yes, sir."

"And how are you finding your schoolwork?" he asked.

"I'm doing okay."

"Excellent, because we wouldn't want to have to hold you back another year."

That was another part of the story. "John" was one year older than Jack and a grade behind, because he'd been ill and missed so much school that he'd failed the year. Jack didn't mind pretending to be older, but he wasn't thrilled about having to seem dumber.

"And how is your health these days?" Mr. McGregor asked.

"I'm fine. It's like I was never sick at all."

"No after-effects of the pneumonia? No lung or breathing problems?"

"None." Jack took a deep breath to prove the point.

"Good." Now he turned to me. "And George."

Thank goodness I got to keep my name. I think it was because nobody was convinced I could remember a new one without slipping up.

"I've been told that you are doing well—"

"Thanks. I'm trying!"

"—with the exception of taking an occasional nap during class time," he said, continuing his thought.

I didn't know what to say.

"It's hard being in a new school," Jack said, jumping to my defence. "Also, we share a room, and I think I snore and keep him awake."

Jack did snore, but that wasn't what was keeping me awake. I somehow couldn't seem to get to sleep very easily. And when I did, I couldn't stay asleep. Sometimes it was because my head was filled with thoughts—about things that had happened to us, things that *could* have happened, how close we'd come to dying, not once or twice but so many times.

"He hasn't fallen asleep too often, has he?" Jack asked.

"It says here," Mr. McGregor said, tapping the file, "that it's happened at least four times."

"I'll try to make sure it doesn't happen again," I offered.

"I think we'd all appreciate that. I know it's not easy being in a new town, new house, new school, with new friends. And of course it must be troubling to have your parents divorce like that."

"Yes, sir."

That was another part of our cover story. Our parents were divorced. That was to explain why my mother— who had worked at the plant before—was now using a different last name. She was now Betty Brown, her maiden name, not Betty Braun. It was only a few letters different so it was easy enough to remember but different enough to avoid detection if anybody was looking through records.

"I think George's trouble sleeping has more to do with being worried about our father," Jack said. "He's serving overseas. He's a pilot."

The final part of our cover: our father was now no longer a soldier serving in Africa; he was a pilot flying out of England.

"You must be very proud of him," Mr. McGregor said. "War is very hard on marriage. Perhaps after the war … who knows?"

"They're talking about getting back together," Jack said. "My mother has let me read some of their letters."

"That's very reassuring."

Starting soon, we'd be getting fake letters delivered from our fake father in England to support our cover. The real letters to and from our real father would be sent through Camp X so they couldn't be traced. It was all part of keeping our cover story alive. None of us was happy about this whole divorce thing—especially not our mother. She said there'd never been a divorce in the history of her family and she wasn't happy to be the first, even if it was all a story. She'd had to take off her engagement and wedding rings. They now sat in a little wooden box on her dresser. A couple of times I'd seen her sitting on her bed, looking at them sadly. I hated to see her so sad.

Part of me thought all of this make-believe was just being paranoid. But then, after what we'd been through, I figured maybe it was better not to take any chances. Worrying about something bad happening—the Nazis or the other bad guys coming after me and Jack and our mom—that's what kept me awake at night, haunted me.

"I'll start sleeping on the couch for a while," Jack offered. "That will help him sleep better so he can stay awake during school."

"That's a generous offer," Mr. McGregor said. "Well, boys," he rose to his feet, "it's been a pleasure to meet you."

"You too, sir," Jack said, and we both stood up to shake his hand.

"And remember, I'm here if either of you boys needs to talk. My door is always open."

"Thank you, sir."

He ushered us out, and the door closed quickly behind us. We were alone. His secretary was nowhere to be seen.

"So much for his door always being open," Jack said under his breath. "We'd better get back to class."

We made our way down the still-empty hall.

"That didn't go so badly," I said.

"Why didn't you tell me you were still having trouble sleeping?" Jack asked.

"It's not as bad as it was before," I lied.

"Still, you should have told me."

"I guess I didn't think you'd care."

"Of course I care. I'm your brother. Maybe you could use some of Mom's sleeping powder."

Our mother had trouble falling asleep and sometimes took a sedative to help. She didn't take it very often, but when she did she was basically unconscious for the night. You could practically bang a drum beside her head and she wouldn't wake up.

"I can't do that without her knowing that I'm having trouble sleeping, and that would only worry her," I said.

"I guess that makes sense. We've worried her enough to last a lifetime. Maybe I *should* sleep on the couch for a while."

"No," I said. "Your snoring really isn't that bad." Another lie. The snoring was bad, but I sort of liked hearing it. I complained about having to share a bedroom with Jack but I liked him being there. Hearing his snoring meant he was close by. Lately, I didn't like being in the house by myself.

"Well, don't fall asleep in class any more," Jack said.

"It's not like I'm trying to fall asleep. It's just that— owww!" I exclaimed. Jack had punched me in the shoulder! "Why did you do that?"

"Just wanted to make sure you would stay awake."

"All right, I'll stay awake!" I protested.

"You'd better. We don't want Mom to get a call from the school about you falling asleep all the time. That'll get her worried for sure." Jack grabbed me by the arm and spun me around so he was looking straight at me. "You understand?"

Jack was older and bigger and stronger than me, but he didn't scare me the way he used to. I'd faced a lot worse than him and survived.

"Well?" he asked again.

I pushed his arm away. "I understand. You keep your paws to yourself."

"You think *you* can tell *me* what—?"

"Is there a problem here?"

We turned around. It was one of the teachers.

"No problem at all," Jack said. He pretended to brush off the front of my shirt with his hands. "My brother had

some crumbs on his shirt left over from lunch. Trying to
tidy him up a bit."

She gave him a look of complete disbelief.

"See you after school, baby brother," he said.

Jack walked off toward his class and I headed for mine.
I knew this wasn't really over, but we were done for now,
at least. I also knew he was right—I sure wasn't going to
be falling asleep for the rest of the day.

CHAPTER THREE

JACK WAS WAITING for me right outside the gates of the school. As soon as I got there he started walking, and I fell in beside him. We walked along in a crowd of other kids, not really with them, more sort of going along in the same direction. There was lots of laughing and joking and talking. It all seemed a little silly. We didn't talk. We just walked. Finally we turned off toward our house and left the others behind.

In the distance we could see the munitions factory. The main building was three or four storeys tall, but there were dozens and dozens of other buildings, some large and some small, stretched out across the grounds, which went on farther than I could see. All around the factory was a tall, barbed-wire fence, with guard towers and gigantic light standards spaced along it. The main gate was two streets over.

18

"I hope you didn't fall asleep this afternoon," Jack said.

"No danger of that. How about you?"

He snorted. "Even if I did they'd probably let me doze. I get the feeling the teacher thinks I'm too dumb to learn anyway."

"You're not dumb," I said.

"Must be if I failed a grade."

"You didn't fail a grade ... it's a cover story."

"You know that, but they don't know it."

"Anyway, you only failed because you were sick, supposedly ... that's why you were held back ... that's the story."

"Yeah, right. If I'd been smart, do you think missing a month of school with pneumonia would have meant taking the whole year again?" he asked.

"I hadn't really thought of that."

"I have. A lot. They think I'm not very bright. And I'm not the only one in my class who's failed. There are at least two others. One of the guys even failed twice.".

"Twice ... wow."

"I'm not sure why he's still in school. He's old enough to drop out and get a job. He could even enlist."

"You have to be eighteen to enlist, don't you?" I asked.

"Seventeen with a letter from your parents."

"That's only a couple more years for you. I guess one more year if your records show you're sixteen instead of fifteen."

"I think Mom knows my real age. I just wish I didn't have to be the stupid brother."

"Would you rather be the sleepy brother?" I said.

"Sleepy beats stupid. Are you making any new friends?"

"I talk to some of the guys, you know, play at recess, but nobody that I'd really want to hang around with after school," I said. "You?"

He shrugged. "Not really. They all seem so young."

"That's because they are young … well, at least compared to you, with you failing a grade and all."

I jumped out of the way, sidestepping Jack's playful swipe at the side of my head.

"I actually know what you're talking about," I said. "Everybody in my class seems like such a *kid*."

Jack laughed. "They are kids. You're only in grade seven."

"You know what I mean. It seems like all they want to talk about is comic books or hockey, or they want to play kids' games like tag or hide-and-go-seek or stupid things like that."

"The sort of games you liked to play a few months ago," Jack said.

"It seems more like a few years ago. So much has happened."

Jack nodded his head. "I don't feel like I have anything in common with anybody my age, either."

"They want to play catch, and I want to play catch-the-spy," I said.

"Me too. Everywhere I look, I see Nazi agents."

"Did you notice that van?" I asked.

"The white one that just passed?"

"Yeah."

"Has it passed us before?"

"No, but if it *did*, I'd notice," I said.

"Me too, I guess. I'm always watching, always waiting for something to happen," Jack said.

"I can't seem to stop watching everything all the time," I said.

"I thought it was only me."

I shook my head. "I'm in school and wondering if my teacher is a Nazi spy."

Jack laughed. "If the Nazis are recruiting sixty-year-old women with pop bottle bottoms for glasses, then we've pretty well won this war."

"A spy could be anybody. You know that," I said. "But it's not just her, it's everybody."

"Yeah, and if you think about it, there *should* be enemy agents here," Jack said. "This is the biggest munitions plant in the entire British Commonwealth, so you have to figure that the Nazis want to infiltrate it. Hitler would love to have this plant destroyed."

That wasn't simply us making things up. Agents who

were training at Camp X tried to break into the plant all the time to test security. We knew that from experience, because *we'd* infiltrated the plant once.

Bill had asked us to do it as part of a test. Really, it was a game he played with the head of security at the plant, Mr. Granger. It happened the first time our mother worked there. We told security that she'd forgotten her lunch, and then we walked right in. If the guards had bothered to look inside the lunch bag they'd have seen that we were carrying a chunk of mud that was supposed to look like some kind of plastic explosive and an alarm clock that was a pretend detonator. We walked right up to Mr. Granger in his office and handed it to him. At the time it seemed like a game. Now it was plain scary. If we could do that, who else could get in?

"Do you think that they might call on us again?" I asked. "Bill?"

"Of course Bill. Or Little Bill." Little Bill was like the top spy, the guy in charge of everything, not only at Camp X but everywhere. "Do you think they might want us for another mission?"

Jack shrugged. "On one hand, I could see them asking us to try to smuggle a fake bomb in again."

"That would make sense. We could do that."

"We could, if they asked us," Jack agreed. "But I'm thinking that probably they're not going to ask us to do anything ever again."

"Why not?"

"Well, they probably don't use kids very often."

"They used us twice, well, really three times," I said.

"But it was always sort of by accident after we'd stumbled into something that we shouldn't have. And I sort of hope we don't stumble into anything here."

"You do?"

"Don't look so surprised," Jack said. "It's probably good for us to go back to being kids again."

I understood what he was saying, but I didn't know if it was possible for us ever to be just kids again.

"I'm spending so much time thinking about things like that, it's like nothing at school seems important," I said. "That's why I can't seem to concentrate."

"Well, you wouldn't have fallen asleep in *my* class this afternoon," Jack said. "We're studying World War I."

"I guess that would be more interesting than math."

"*Everything* is more interesting than math. Do you know what they used to call that war?" Jack asked.

"The Great War," I said, feeling smugly satisfied.

"That was one of the names. They also called it 'the War to End All Wars.'"

I laughed. "That didn't work."

"It was the War to End All Wars for less than twenty years," Jack said. "Today, we learned about the Halifax Explosion."

I gave him a questioning look.

"It happened in 1917. Like now, back then they made explosives and ammunition here in Canada and shipped them over to Europe for the war. There was this ship in the Halifax harbour and it was loaded with explosives, ammunition, and it was hit by another ship. It caught fire."

"Wow, that would have been something to see."

"That was part of the problem. Hundreds and hundreds of people came to see it burning in the harbour. And then, when it exploded, the impact was so huge that they were all killed. A thousand people died instantly, and then another thousand died of their injuries within the next two days."

"Unbelievable," I gasped.

"There were over nine thousand people injured, including more than a hundred who were blinded."

"By the flash?" I questioned.

"Flying glass. They were standing behind windows, watching, and when it blew, the windows shattered and shards of glass shot into their eyes."

I cringed at the thought.

"Almost every building within a mile of the explosion was flattened, and there were fires everywhere in the wreckage. The streets were on fire. A lot of people were trapped and burned alive."

Again, another terrible thought.

"Hot fragments of metal fell from the sky. When it rained the next day, the rain was black, but at least it helped put out the fires. And the anchor of the ship, which weighed over eleven hundred pounds, was found two and a half miles inland."

"Two and a half miles?" I gasped. "No way."

"They felt the explosion a hundred miles away. It shook things on shelves. They said the fireball was a mile high. It was the largest explosion of all time."

I nodded my head in amazement. "And that was all from just one ship."

"One big ship," Jack said.

"But it was still *one* ship. How much in the way of explosives do you think are here at the plant?"

"I don't know, but it's the biggest plant anywhere. There might be ten or twenty or even a hundred times as much explosives as there were on that ship," Jack said.

"And our house is less than a half mile from the plant."

"A lot less," Jack confirmed.

Jack and I were both thinking the same thing, trying to imagine what would happen if the plant exploded.

"If this plant blew up it would make the Halifax Explosion look like a firecracker," I said.

"Yeah, but they have lots of safety features, and the plant has lots of separate buildings so fires or explosions would be contained," Jack said.

"And that makes you feel safer?"

He shook his head. "I've never liked Mom working there."

"It seems sort of silly to worry about what could happen when she's at work," I said.

"What's silly about that?" Jack asked. "It *is* dangerous. Something *could* happen."

"Yeah, but it's not just when she's at work. If you think about it, she's in danger when she's sleeping in her bed at home, too," I said.

Jack shrugged. "I guess we're all in danger. It would be one heck of an explosion."

Great. None of this was going to make getting to sleep tonight any easier.

CHAPTER FOUR

"THANKS FOR DINNER, Mom," I said.

"You're very welcome."

I stood up, picked up my plate and carried it to the kitchen.

"I'm sorry I can't help clean up," my mother said. She looked up at the clock on the kitchen wall. "My shift starts in less than thirty minutes."

"That's okay. We can handle it," Jack replied.

"I've learned that you boys can handle most anything. Are you going to go to the Community Hall this evening?"

"We were thinking about it," Jack said.

"You should. They're going to be showing a movie, plus a couple of cartoons and a newsreel. It should be good fun."

"I guess we'll go."

"I really think you should. It's important for you boys to go out and spend time with other people your age, make some new friends. Maybe then you wouldn't fight with each other so much."

"We don't fight!" Jack protested, before he realized that it was way too big a lie to get away with. "Well, not that much."

"No more than we ever did," I agreed. "We're brothers. We're supposed to fight."

"I just remember when our house was always filled with your friends," she said.

"That didn't stop us from fighting," I pointed out.

"And that was back home, with our *real* friends," Jack said.

"The kids here are as real as the ones back home."

"You know what I mean," Jack argued. "It's different with people you've known since you were little."

"Yes, but it's like planting a tree. The best way to eventually have an old friend is to make a new one. You two can make new friends. There are so many new people at the plant, there must be lots and lots of new kids as well."

"Seems like there are more every day," I confirmed.

"Right, so it's not like you're the only new kids at school, trying to break into a group of people who've known each other for years," she pointed out.

That was true.

"Then you should try to make some friends. Promise me you'll try."

We both reluctantly mumbled something that sounded like agreement.

"Good!" she exclaimed. "Now, I'd better be off. I don't want to be late for my shift." She gave us each a kiss on the cheek and then headed out the door. "And I expect both of you to be in bed and sound asleep when I get home tonight."

"We will be," Jack said.

I could agree to the "in bed" part, but being asleep I couldn't guarantee. Actually, I could practically guarantee the opposite. I didn't like to even try to sleep until I heard the front door open and I knew Mom was home. I really didn't feel great about her walking home alone in the dark. There were too many things that could happen to her—too much that *had* happened to her—and I needed to know she was safe. I would stay in bed, lights off, lying still, just waiting.

Besides, I'd got to the point that I was almost afraid to fall sleep. The last few nights I'd had the same nightmare—me in a tunnel and the walls closing in and then collapsing, and being buried, suffocating and ... I shook it off. Bad enough that I dreamed it—I didn't want to think about it when I was awake, too.

*   *   *

We walked up to the main gate of the plant. Like a lot of things in town, the Community Hall was actually on the factory grounds, and movie night was an event for plant employees and their families.

"Looks familiar, eh?" Jack said.

"Maybe a little too familiar."

The last time—the *only* time—we'd walked through that gate was to deliver the fake bomb, three months ago. In some ways that seemed like only yesterday. In other ways it was more like a hundred years ago—no, more like a dream or a movie I'd seen, definitely not something that had actually happened to Jack and me.

"Do you think it'll be the same guards?" Jack asked.

"I hope not."

"Why?"

"Because they might recognize us," I said.

Jack snorted. "First off, it was a long time ago. Second, we're not that memorable. Third, those guards are so old that they probably wouldn't recognize us if it had happened yesterday. And, finally, so what if they did?"

"But we smuggled a fake bomb into the——" I stopped myself as I realized what he meant. They didn't know what we'd done. Nobody at the plant except for the head of security, Mr. Granger, knew anything about what had happened, and Bill had told us that Mr. Granger had been "briefed" on us being here again.

We stopped in front of the gatehouse. There were only a few entrances into the plant and each was guarded, the road blocked by a long metal rail that needed to be lifted to allow any traffic to pass.

"Good evening, boys," the guard said as he walked toward us. His rifle was slung over his back.

"Good evening, sir," we both answered.

He was old, like all the guards at the plant. It was rare to see young men—anybody between eighteen and forty—anywhere. They'd all enlisted and were overseas fighting the Nazis. Like our father. That meant that older men—men who were too old to fight in this war—were responsible for military duties that didn't involve combat. They were members of what was called the Veteran Guard. Some were in their late-fifties or sixties, and a lot of them were men who had fought in World War I. Some of the guard detail at Camp 30, the prisoner-of-war camp, had looked as though they were too old to have fought in World War I. It hadn't filled me with confidence to see those guys guarding the prisoners. No more than it gave me confidence to see them guarding this plant.

"State your business," the guard said very formally. "And speak up ... I'm a little deaf in the one ear."

"We're here to see a movie," Jack said. "Our mother works here."

"And who's your mother?" he asked.

"Betty Brown."

It caught me a little by surprise. I wasn't used to her name being Brown. At least we still got to be Brauns, though our "divorced" mother had gone back to her maiden name.

"Is she new here?" he asked.

"A few weeks."

"That practically makes her a veteran. Do you know how many new people have started here in the last month?" he asked.

"A lot, I guess."

"I could tell you, but it's classified information. Let's just say more than a lot. Was a time when I knew everybody who lived around here. Then I only knew all the people at the plant. Now?" He shrugged and shook his head. "Let me have a look at my list."

He pulled a book out of his inside pocket, opened it up and started flipping through the pages. Settling on one, he scanned down it. Finally he looked up at us through his thick glasses. "I don't see no Betty Black in here."

"It's Betty *Brown*," Jack said.

"Brown?"

"Yes. Betty Brown, not Black."

"Why didn't you say that in the first place?"

"We did say Brown!" Jack exclaimed. "Do you think that we don't know our own mother's name?"

The guard started flipping through the pages again, ignoring Jack's question. He ran his finger down a page.

"Here it is, Betty Brown. But it doesn't say anything about any kids, and I can't let you in unless you're listed in this book."

"Betty Brown is our mother. Our last name is Braun. George and Jack ... I mean John Braun."

The security guard looked at him questioningly. "You sure you got your first name right this time? Is it John or Jack?"

"It's both," Jack protested. "It's officially John, but people call me Jack."

"How come you have a different name than your mother?" the guard questioned.

"Our parents are divorced," I said.

"Divorced? In my day, a man and a woman stayed together no matter what. 'What God has joined together let no man put asunder,' and all that."

I could feel Jack getting ready to explode.

"Our father is in Africa fighting—"

"He *was* in Africa," Jack said, cutting me off.

I'd forgotten about the cover story. "Yeah, now he's in Europe with the air force. He's a Spitfire pilot. He's shot down six Nazi planes," I said. That was all part of the cover story.

"Good for him. You must be proud of him. Still, I don't

see your names here," the guard said. "No John or George or Jack Brown is on my list to admit."

"We're not Brown. We're Braun!" Jack exclaimed. "Remember? We have a different name than our mother."

"Oh, yeah, of course, don't know where my head is. Say … Braun … isn't that a German name?"

Again I felt Jack start to bristle, so I jumped in. "Our grandfather was German. We're Canadians."

The guard shrugged. "Makes no difference to me. They're so desperate for workers I think they might hire Adolf Hitler himself if he'd promise to show up, work hard and not take any matches or lighters onto the grounds." He looked at us again. "Do you boys have any matches or lighters?"

"Of course not," Jack said.

"Just have to be careful. Better safe than sorry." He looked back down at the list. "Here we go, John and George Braun. You're on the list. Please proceed."

"Thank you," I said. "Come on, John."

We walked past the gatehouse. There were two other guards sitting inside. They were both considerably younger, almost young enough not to be members of the Veteran Guard. We waved, and they waved back to us as we passed.

"That was unbelievable," Jack said as we continued to walk. "We could have brought anything in. He didn't search us, he didn't check us—"

"He did look at the list until he found our names," I said, defending him.

"But he didn't know if we actually were who we said we were. We could have claimed to be anybody."

"I hadn't thought of that."

"Somebody should. Maybe we should talk to Bill," Jack suggested.

"Maybe we should just go and see a movie."

"Bill should know."

"Bill probably already knows. Besides, do you even know how to get in touch with him?" I asked.

"Well … I guess we could go up to Camp X."

"No, we can't. We're not supposed to go there any more," I said, reminding him of what Bill had told us. "How about if we go to the movie? Do you know where the Community Hall is?"

"It's this way," he said. "Some of the kids from my class told me how to find it. You're right, let's go and watch a movie."

CHAPTER FIVE

IT FELT GOOD sitting in the dark, watching the images up on the screen. We got two Looney Tunes cartoons— one a Daffy Duck and the other a Bugs Bunny. He really was a *wascally wabbit*. They made me laugh so hard that I forgot about everything—not just here, but everywhere.

And that's when the newsreel came on. No cartoon. No pretend. It showed film that had been taken of our soldiers. A lot of it was troops waving and smiling, and then maps and arrows so we'd know some of what was happening. But it also showed some burned-out tanks and German prisoners of war, hands on their heads, being marched away under armed guard.

It didn't say where it was but the background looked like desert, all scrub and hardly any vegetation. It could have been North Africa, where our real father really was. There had obviously been a big battle, and if we'd killed and captured some of their men there was every possibility that they'd killed and captured some of ours ... maybe even ... I couldn't think about that. There was no point. I had to believe that he was all right and if something had happened they'd let us know. But how long would it take before we found out? Would it be days, or weeks? Could my father have been in that battle, and we were watching the film of what happened before we actually knew what had happened to him? Again, I couldn't let my head go there any more.

The newsreel ended and the screen went dark. I tried to keep up with news of the war, but right now it was almost more than I could handle. Maybe no news was the best news. Cartoons and movies were about all I wanted to see right now.

The screen came to life and the title of the movie flashed across it, *Gone with the Wind*.

"Shoot, figures the only movie we've seen in the last two months is the one they're showing tonight," Jack muttered. He got to his feet.

"Wait!" I grabbed him by the arm. "We could see it again."

"Nah, I know how it ends. Besides, it wasn't like it was a good movie or anything. The war part was hardly mentioned. It was mainly a stupid love story and—"

"Boys!" a woman said, turning around in her seat. "Please, we're trying to watch the movie!"

"And I'm trying to leave it," Jack said. He brushed my hand away and shuffled down the row.

Just because *he* didn't want to see the movie didn't mean that *I* didn't want to see it. It was a good movie … except for the romantic stuff. At least it was better than nothing. Beside, he couldn't tell me what to do. He wasn't the boss of me. Maybe I'd stay and watch the movie by myself.

I turned and watched as he walked up the aisle. The back door opened, letting in a shaft of light, and Jack exited to the lobby. The door closed behind him and the light was gone. Suddenly I didn't want to see the movie so much.

"Excuse me," I said, stumbling and tripping and stepping on toes as I went after him.

I ran up the aisle and through the door, and Jack was standing right there at the candy counter. He turned around. He was holding a bag of peanuts and a bag of popcorn.

"A peace offering. Your choice," he said, holding them both out.

I took the popcorn.

"I just didn't want to see it," he said. "You can go back in and watch it if you want. I'll even come back and get you at the end."

"I can get home by myself," I said. "It's not like I don't know the way."

"I know. But Mom might not be happy if she knew I'd left you here."

"Well then maybe you shouldn't tell her," I suggested.

"It's not me I'm worried about doing the blabbing." He leaned in close. "Can't you get it straight where our father is stationed?" he whispered.

"It's hard to get everything right," I said. "At least I know what my name is, *John*."

Jack looked embarrassed.

"Do you *really* want to see the movie?" he asked.

I shook my head. "Let me finish my popcorn and we can head home."

"That's a—"

"Excuse me."

It was a woman ... well, a girl, sort of. Her hair was all done up with hairspray and she was chewing on a wad of gum. She was wearing makeup—what my mother would have called *too much* makeup—and some really strong perfume.

"My girlfriends and I," she said, gesturing to two others who were about her age and equally made up, "we have a bet as to how old you are."

"What?" Jack asked. He looked even more embarrassed now.

"We were wondering how old you are," she repeated.

Before he could answer, she waved the others over, and

they came and joined us. We were suddenly engulfed in a cloud of thick, stinky perfume. It wasn't just that I could smell it, I could *taste* it.

"So how old is he, Daphne?" one of the two others said, and giggled.

"He hasn't told me yet. He's playing hard to get."

Hard to get? He wasn't playing anything.

"We were thinking that you aren't eighteen," the first girl, Daphne, said.

"Because we figured that a big guy like you would have joined the army if he was eighteen," one of the others added.

"You can bet on that," Jack said. "I'm going to enlist on my birthday. I'll be standing there at the recruiting office waiting for them to open the door in the morning."

"So how old are you?" Daphne asked.

"How old are you three?" Jack asked.

"We asked first."

"Well, I'm not saying anything until you tell me your ages."

"A gentleman never asks a lady her age," she said, and she giggled again.

"If you were ladies in the first place you wouldn't have been asking me *my* age," Jack said.

"Oh, we have ourselves a live one here!" one of the others said, and all three started to giggle.

"Okay, you win. We'll tell you," Daphne said. "Juliette has just turned eighteen."

Juliette curtsied slightly. She was wearing thick red lipstick to go along with her extra-heavy makeup. I wondered if she'd used a putty knife to apply it.

"And Doris is almost nineteen."

"In two weeks," she said, "although you don't have to get me a present if you don't want to."

"And you?" Jack asked.

"I'm the baby. I won't be eighteen until next spring."

"Which would make you seventeen," Jack said.

Funny, she didn't look seventeen—she looked older than either of the other two.

"Which is *my* bet as to how old *you* are," Daphne said.

"And you two ... how old do you think I am?" Jack asked.

"We both thought you must be sixteen," Doris said, and Juliette nodded in agreement.

"Well, you only missed by one year," Jack said.

The hair on the back of my head stood up—had Jack now forgotten how old he was *supposed* to be? They'd guessed right as far as the world was concerned.

"That's right, he's seventeen," I said, jumping in before Jack could say fifteen.

Jack looked at me and his eyes widened ever so slightly in surprise, before he realized that he'd almost told them he was fifteen and blown his cover.

"The same age as *me*," Daphne said, sounding pleased.

"And almost our age," Doris protested.

"Yeah, what's a year among friends?" Juliette asked.

Jack looked pleased and embarrassed at the same time. "You said you had a bet … what was it for?"

All three girls giggled.

"What was the bet for?" he asked again.

"Well … it's just that … you know … there really aren't that many males around here," Daphne said.

"Unless you count men who are old enough to be our grandfathers," Doris said.

"Or kids," Juliette added. "And the few men in between seem to be married or injured or jerks."

"So … the winner gets to buy you a soda," Daphne said. "Do you want a soda to go along with those peanuts?"

"Sure … I guess," Jack said.

"We all just started working at the plant," Daphne said, "but none of us have seen you around."

"I haven't seen *you* around either," he said.

"That's not surprising," Doris said. "There are so many people who work here."

"Ten thousand," Juliette said.

"That's nine thousand people more than the whole town where I grew up in northern Ontario," Doris said.

"So, which section do you work in?" Daphne asked.

"I don't work here," he said.

"Where do you work?"

"I'm in school," he said, looking down at the floor. "High school."

"So he's a smart one, too," Juliette said.

"Sure beats the heck out of working around here!" Daphne exclaimed.

"I'm only staying in school until I'm old enough to enlist," Jack added.

"And how about you?" Juliette asked me. "You wouldn't happen to be seventeen as well, would you?"

"Me?"

"Yeah, I was thinking a really *short* seventeen. Or maybe sixteen. Sixteen would be okay."

"I'm twelve!" I exclaimed.

"I guess that is a little young." She paused. "When do you turn thirteen?"

"Juliette!" Doris shrieked, and Daphne and Jack both laughed. "That's not proper!"

"What? He's the second most eligible male I've seen tonight." She reached over, stuck her hand in my popcorn bag and took some. "Look at him," she said, "you have to admit that he is cute."

"And *twelve*," Doris said.

"I was thinking we could be friends for three or four years, until he turns sixteen."

"And you'll be twenty-one," Daphne added.

"Oh, my goodness, by then I'll practically be an old maid." She turned back to me. "So, when is your birthday?"

"July tenth."

"Oh, that's so perfect! I've always wanted a summer wedding!"

There was a gale of laughter that Jack joined in on, and it felt as though every pair of eyes in the lobby was now looking at us.

"Here, take this," I said as I pressed my bag of popcorn into Daphne's hands.

"I was hoping for an engagement ring, but this is a start," she said, and everybody laughed again.

I turned and rushed away, heading to the safety of the men's washroom.

"I'm just kidding, honey!" she called after me. "We don't have to get married right away!"

There was more laughter. Now I *knew* everybody was looking at us. I pushed the door open and quickly closed it behind me.

I took a deep breath and looked around. Thank goodness I was alone ... wasn't I? There were two stalls. There was nobody at either of the urinals and the doors to the two stalls were partially open. I pushed one open and then the other. Nobody in either.

High above the sink was a window, propped open. If I climbed up on the sink I could reach it, and it was definitely big enough for me to get through. I could lower myself down to the ground below and escape and … no, that was plain stupid.

I turned on the cold-water tap and splashed some water on my burning cheeks. Maybe I wasn't going to climb out through the window, but that didn't mean I had to walk out any time soon. I went over to one of the stalls and closed the door behind me, making sure it was securely locked. I didn't have to go, but this was as good a place as any to sit and wait.

Then, as I sat there, I realized how silly this was. I'd faced Nazi agents, been tied up, hit on the head, kidnapped and threatened with death, and here I was sitting in a stall in the washroom because some girl— some *stupid* girl—had said some things that were embarrassing. Really, they should have been embarrassing to *her*. I wasn't the one acting all goofy and saying silly things. The only reason she'd gone on and on was because she knew it was getting to me. Well, I'd show her.

I got up, opened the stall and marched toward the door. I stopped for a brief second, took a deep breath, and then walked out into the lobby and … I didn't see her, or the other girls, or Jack. There were people standing at the counter waiting for popcorn or candy or soda, but none of those four was anywhere to be seen. The girls must have gone into the movie, and Jack must have gone home.

Great, I'd have to walk home by myself. Well, at least I wouldn't have to put up with what he was going to say to me. No doubt he'd enjoyed the whole humiliating scene.

"George!"

I turned around. A woman—a very old woman—working the candy counter waved me over. Who was she, and why did she know my name? She'd probably overheard the whole conversation.

"This is for you," she said. She pushed a soda and a big bag of popcorn across the counter.

"For me?"

She nodded. "From your brother. He paid for them and told me to look out for you."

"Where *is* my brother?"

"He went into the movie."

"But he didn't want to see that movie."

"He went in with those three young ladies."

My eyes widened slightly in shock.

"He said you should join them."

"Yeah, like that's going to happen." I took the popcorn and soda and walked away. I wanted to sit down somewhere and think things through. I looked around. There was no place to sit. Actually, in a theatre there were hundreds of places to sit ... and I *did* want to see the movie. I would go back in. But I wasn't going to be sitting anywhere near them.

CHAPTER SIX

"I DON'T KNOW why you're so mad," Jack said as we walked home in the dark.

"Who says I'm mad?"

"You haven't said a word to me since we left the movie."

"Maybe I only talk when I actually have something to say. That's an idea your new friends might want to think about."

"They were only pulling your leg, George. Don't be such a whiny little baby."

"Better than being a stupid, giggling schoolgirl."

"They're not schoolgirls."

"No, I was talking about you. You should have heard yourself, Jack, giggling and laughing at every stupid thing they said. I can't believe they don't think you're seven instead of seventeen."

"Hey, that wasn't my fault!" Jack protested. "It wasn't me who told them I was seventeen!"

"Yeah, you're the one who was going to tell them you're fifteen and blow your cover ... you *idiot*."

Jack grabbed me by the arm and spun me around. Maybe calling him names wasn't the smartest thing to do.

"Who are you calling an idiot?" he demanded, staring me down.

There were only two possible things to do now, and I didn't feel like doing the apologizing one because I wasn't sorry.

"I guess the idiot who couldn't keep his cover story straight, so that would be you."

I waited for him to do something, take a shot at me, but he didn't.

"And telling them I was seventeen didn't break my cover story either?" he said. "I'm only supposed to be sixteen, so who's the idiot now?"

"You're still the idiot. A guy might lie and say he's older because he's trying to impress some dame, but he wouldn't lie and say he's younger."

I brushed his arm away and turned and started walking again.

"Look, at least they apologized to you."

I had to admit that they had done that.

"I told them they had to," Jack said.

"You did?"

"Yeah. I told them the only one allowed to pick on my little brother was me."

That sounded like something Jack would say.

"Did you see Mr. Granger?" he asked.

"I saw him."

Mr. Granger had been standing outside the Community Hall when we'd left, off to the side, watching everybody.

"Do you think he saw us?" Jack asked.

"He and I made eye contact, and he gave me a little smile and a nod before he turned away," I said.

"I guess he can't do anything more than that."

"Nope. He has no reason to know us, and if he talked he'd be jeopardizing our cover."

Mr. Granger could certainly blow our cover, because he knew us from before. But Bill had told us once that he'd trust Mr. Granger with his life, so that was good enough for me. Funny, with him being in charge of security at a place filled with explosives, where our mother worked, right beside where we lived, I guess we *were* trusting him with our lives.

"Owww!" I screamed as Jack punched me in the arm. "What was that for?"

"That was for calling me an idiot ... even if I was one."

*   *   *

I turned over and flopped down in the bed, trying to get more comfortable. I took the pillow and folded it over so it was twice as thick and put it under my head. It was too dark to see the clock but it had to be close to one by now. I'd heard Mom come in at about twelve-thirty, and that was at least half an hour ago, maybe longer.

I could still hear her moving around in the kitchen. She had her own sleep problems. She'd had them since our father had shipped overseas. I knew she was worried about him, the same way I was worried about him *and* her. Sometimes she'd go three or four days with hardly any sleep. You could see it in her face. Then she'd finally give in and use some of that sleeping powder, and at last she'd get a good, solid rest. Those nights a tank could have rolled through our house and she wouldn't have noticed. I wished she'd use that powder more often, but she said she didn't want to get "dependent" on it.

Her moving around, things moving around in my head and Jack snoring—all were working to keep me awake. And Jack's snoring was getting worse. Maybe I needed to ask him to move to the chesterfield for a few days.

The door to the bedroom opened a crack. A thin line of light appeared, and then the silhouette of my mother as she peered in. I closed my eyes and lay perfectly still—I wanted to make sure that she didn't know I was still awake. There was no point in worrying her any more about my sleep problems.

Her checking on us was a good sign. That was one of the last things she did every night before she went to sleep herself. After that, I knew I'd be able to drift off. Maybe. At least with it being Friday night I didn't have to get up early for school. I could even have a nap tomorrow, if I wanted to. So could Mom. And starting Monday she'd be on day shift, which meant I could get to sleep earlier for the next two weeks because I wouldn't be worried about her coming in so late.

I heard the front door open and my ears perked up. Why would she open the front door? Maybe she was checking to see that it was locked. I heard it close again.

Sometimes I'd get up in the middle of the night to check it myself. Then I'd go and look in on my mother to make sure she was in her bed asleep. I knew that was silly, but I had to look. I'd stand there in her doorway, stock-still, hidden in the dark, holding my breath, listening until I heard her softly breathing or saw a slight movement in her bed that let me know she was there and everything was fine.

I heard footsteps outside ... or did I? They were very faint. Probably it was only somebody walking by. But whatever was out there—if it was anything more than my imagination—was now gone. Either way, there was nothing I could do about it. I needed to turn over and get to sleep … but I was more awake now than ever. Maybe I still needed to get up and check the door myself.

Quietly I climbed out of bed. Moving silently on bare feet I padded out of my room, using one hand against the wall to steady and guide me. Across the living room, light shone in through the front window and lit my way to the door. I jiggled the handle ever so slightly. It was locked all right. As expected. I could go to sleep now. Or maybe I should just look in on my mother. But she might still be awake, and then she'd ask me why I was still awake. I could tell her I was going to the washroom.

It was only a few steps to her bedroom. Her door was open and the lights were out. I peeked in around the corner and looked and listened. I couldn't see anything, and the only thing I could hear was my heart pounding in my ears. Was she even in bed? But where else could she be? I looked around. Obviously she wasn't in the living room, and the bathroom door was open and the light was out so she wasn't there. The kitchen was dark as well. This was one of the few advantages of living in such a small house. She *had* to be in bed.

I took a small step into my mother's room. I didn't want to startle her but I had to see. I stopped and listened again. Nothing. No sound. And while I saw something in her bed—a dark shape—it really didn't look big enough to be her. I went closer and closer, turning my head to listen. Finally I stood right over her bed. I reached down and took the corner of the blanket and pulled it away. There were two pillows in the bed where she should have been.

CHAPTER SEVEN

"EARTH TO GEORGE."

I started at Jack's voice. "Yeah?"

"The pancakes," he said.

I looked down at the platter of pancakes sitting beside me.

"Pass the pancakes, you little goof."

"Jack, there's no need for you to talk to your brother like that."

"Well, I wouldn't have to if he'd passed them the first time I asked."

"Sorry, didn't hear you," I said.

"Did you sleep all right last night?" my mother asked.

"I slept okay," I lied. "How about you?"

"I slept like a baby," she said. "I was asleep soon after I got home."

I looked at her. That was a lie, but she was telling it so

well that if I hadn't known it was a lie I never would have suspected.

"Really? That's great, because I know you usually have trouble getting to sleep right away when you've been on swing shift," I said.

"Well, last night was different."

"Did you take your sleeping powder?" Jack asked.

"I didn't need to. You boys worry too much about me. I'm the mother and you're the children ... remember?"

"We remember," Jack said. "Speaking of which, I was thinking, if I could have *my mother's* permission, I'd like to go to the Community Hall tonight and play bingo."

"Since when do you like playing bingo?" my mother asked.

Exactly what I was wondering myself!

"It's not really that I like bingo, but I promised some friends."

"What type of friends?" my mother asked. There was a smile in her voice.

"Just friends." Jack looked embarrassed.

"Girl friends?"

"They're girls who are my friends, if that's what you mean," he protested. "You told us we should make new friends."

"I did. Are these girls from school?"

"I met them last night at the movies," Jack said.

I noticed how he'd answered her question without answering it. He looked over at me. He was wondering if I was going to give it away. I was pretty sure he didn't want her to know that they were actual *women* who worked in the plant, not girls from his school.

"Sure," Mom said, "go have fun tonight playing bingo with the girls who are friends but not necessarily *girl-friends*." Wow, if I'd teased him like that I'd have gotten a punch in the arm. "Now, how about if you two do me a favour?" she asked.

"That depends on the favour," Jack said.

"I promised Mrs. Edwards down the street that I'd look in on her this morning. I'd like you to finish the dishes while I'm gone."

"That we can do," Jack offered.

She gave him a little hug and then gave me a kiss on the top of my head. She took her jacket from the hook and was gone. Now it was just Jack and me, and I finally had a chance to tell him what had happened last night.

Jack was already clearing off the table.

"Mom was lying," I said.

"She's not going to see Mrs. Edwards?"

"I don't know anything about Mrs. Edwards. I mean about going right to sleep last night."

"That didn't sound right to me, either," Jack agreed. "It

usually takes her a long time to get to sleep ... she was probably tossing and turning in her bed for hours."

"She wasn't *in* her bed," I said. "She left the house about one-thirty and she didn't get back for almost an hour."

Jack gave me a questioning look.

"I couldn't sleep either and I heard her go out. I stayed awake until she got home."

"And where did she go?"

"It's not like I asked her. When I heard her unlock the front door I jumped into bed so she wouldn't know that I knew she'd been out."

"She probably went out for a walk."

"In the middle of the night?" I asked.

"People who can't get to sleep do things like that. Besides, what other reason could there be?"

I shrugged. I couldn't think of one.

"Unless you think she was out being a Nazi spy. Do you think our mother is an enemy agent, Georgie?" He flicked me in the back with the dishcloth.

"But then why did she tell us she was sleeping?" I asked. "Why would she lie to us?"

"I don't know. She probably didn't want us to worry about her sleep problems."

"Maybe. But I don't like being lied to," I said. "And Mom doesn't like it either. Which reminds me, you're not going to tell her about your new friends, are you?"

"What's to tell?"

"Oh, I don't know, maybe that they're way older than you?"

"They're not that much older. I'm almost sixteen … almost seventeen, according to my school records and everything that everybody here knows."

"You're closer to fifteen than you are to sixteen, and I think Mom knows your real age."

"Yeah, but it's like what we were talking about. I don't have anything in common with kids my real age."

"And what exactly do you have in common with those three?" I asked. "Besides the fact that they're older, they work and you go to school, they live in dormitories and you live with your mommy."

"Well, you don't have to spend time with them," Jack said. "I like Daphne and she likes me."

"She likes the seventeen-year-old you."

"And that's the one she's going to get."

"What if she finds out you're not seventeen? What if Mom finds out you're going out with somebody who's two years older than you?"

"Only two people know those things—me and you. And I'm not telling anybody, and neither are you."

"I might keep it all a secret."

"Might?' Jack asked.

"It depends on how a certain person treats his little brother."

"If you're not careful, the doctor is going to be treating you for a broken arm."

"And unless you're going to break my face too, then Mom is going to find out who broke my arm and why he did it. So maybe you're the one who needs to be careful."

Jack tried to stare me down. I didn't look away.

"Besides, it's not me you have to worry about," I said. "In case you haven't noticed, they all work in the same plant."

"Along with ten thousand other people. They're not on the same line, or in the same building, or even on the same shift," Jack said. "And can you imagine our mother sharing a coffee break with any of those girls?"

That thought made me smile.

"So, you keep your mouth closed and I'll keep my fist open. Agreed?"

We shook hands on it.

"Under the B ... fifteen!" the announcer called out.

I looked at my card. No fifteen. I hadn't won all night, but that wasn't surprising considering how many people were playing. There had to be close to two hundred people, and some of them were playing three or four bingo cards at the same time.

The few males in the room were either really young—
kids from our school—or really old. The women were
mostly about my mother's age, but there were younger
ones too, like Daphne, and some who were old enough to
be grandmothers or maybe great-grandmothers.

I was sitting by myself, and Juliette and Daphne were
sitting with Jack on the far side of the room. Juliette had
started to give me a hard time again, kidding me about
the two of us dating. I'd told her that it wouldn't be
happening because I needed somebody who was "more
mature." After everybody stopped laughing at her, she
decided to leave me alone.

"Under the G … fifty-four!"

Again, no luck.

"Bingo!" somebody yelled out, and a chorus of groans
came from around the room.

"Please wait until we check the card," the announcer
said.

That was just a formality. A runner went to check out
the card.

I looked over at Jack. He and Daphne were practically
intertwined, they were sitting so close together. On the
way over he'd told me that he didn't want me to sit close
to them. That wasn't a problem for me. Between her
perfume and his aftershave—our *father's* aftershave—
there was practically a haze over their table. Wasn't there

some sort of rule that you had to shave before you could use aftershave?

Even more nauseating than the smell was the conversation. Between the giggling—and Jack was doing his share of that—there was a steady stream of stupidity. And it wasn't just the girls. Jack seemed to have lost half his brain on the walk over.

That was enough for me. I'd played my final card. I drained the last of my soda and headed out. I wanted to get some fresh air. I thought about letting Jack know I was leaving but I didn't think he'd notice or miss me.

I walked over to the side of the building where I knew there was a bench, but skidded to a stop when I saw it was already occupied. I really wanted to find someplace to be alone. I circled around to the back where there was a set of steps to sit on. There was no one there. It was darker, away from the lights, but that was okay. I wasn't afraid of the dark. After all the noise of the bingo game it was nice to sit out in the quiet.

"How are you?"

I jumped, and my head swivelled around. There was the darkened silhouette of a man standing in the shadows, the red glow of a cigarette in his hand.

"I didn't mean to surprise you." His voice sounded familiar.

"That's okay. I just didn't see you there."

"Really? I thought you'd followed *me* out here, George."

"Me? I wasn't following any ..." He'd called me George. Who did I know that knew me who would be here tonight?

"I figured you might have been given a lesson on tailing people by Bill."

My heart leapt up into my throat. Whoever it was knew Bill. There was hardly anybody ... except for maybe ...

"Mr. Granger?"

He stepped out from the shadows and I could see his face. It *was* Mr. Granger!

"I'm so glad to see you!"

"It's good to see you, too." He gave me a curious look. "So, you weren't following me?"

"I didn't notice you out here. And I didn't notice you inside before that. I guess I was too busy playing bingo."

"And your brother was too busy playing footsies with that young lady. She started working here recently, isn't that right?"

"Yeah."

"She must be fairly young, but still a few years older than your brother."

"A couple ... well, one year older ... you know."

He nodded. "Cover story. There are so many young women working here and so few young men that it doesn't surprise me that one of them has pounced on your brother. You should be careful, you might be next."

"I'll keep my eyes open for that."

"Keeping your eyes open is a large part of my job. The head of security has to watch everything, all the time. Although that's getting harder to do."

"What with the new people being hired, right?"

"Exactly. Despite the fact that I'm practically living here these days, I can't keep up with all the new employees being added."

"But they must have given you some new guards, too," I said.

"They've added more *old* guards."

Of course I knew what he meant—most of his security people were members of the Veteran Guard.

"Some of them are the most dedicated old soldiers you'd ever want to meet. I'd trust them with my life. Makes me understand how we won the First World War. Others are just old. And with so much going on around here it would be helpful to have a couple of extra pairs of eyes at work."

"I guess every little bit helps," I agreed.

"I sometimes wish I could get a couple of pairs of *young* eyes to help out."

"Young?"

"Like you and Jack," he said. "I know you two don't miss much."

I shook my head. "We can't do that."

"I know," he said. "At least, not without the permission of Camp X."

"And our mother," I said. "I don't think there's any way she'd ever let us do anything like that ever again."

"No?"

"No way. She doesn't like any of this spy stuff."

He nodded his head, but there was a strange glint in his eyes, like he really didn't believe me.

"You'd better get back in there," Mr. Granger said. "Nobody should see the two of us talking. Not good for your cover."

I nodded my head and started to walk away, and then stopped and turned back around. "Mr. Granger," I called out. "If we did see something … not that we're looking for trouble or anything … we'd tell you."

"I know you would. Say hello to your brother and mother for me."

I'd say hello to Jack, but I thought it was best to keep this whole conversation a secret from my mother.

CHAPTER EIGHT

SOMEHOW IT SEEMED easier to lie in bed with my eyes wide open. I was *trying* to stay awake, not fall asleep, but that way, if I fell asleep it would be okay—but if I stayed awake, I was doing what I was trying to do. It was definitely better than tossing and turning and *trying* to go to sleep.

I'd made a decision five days ago that I wasn't going to go to sleep at night until I was sure that my mother was not only home but also in bed sleeping. After I was sure she was in her bed and asleep, every night I'd check that the front door was locked. If she went for another "walk" late at night I was going to follow her. Obviously I didn't tell my mother my plan, but I also kept it from Jack.

Not that he'd have noticed. He had been out three or four times with Daphne, and whenever he was home, he really wasn't. His mind was elsewhere. He'd also been treating me better. I wasn't sure if that was because he was "in love" or because he'd realized that he had to keep up his end of the deal so I'd help him keep his secret. Either way, I didn't think it would last long.

Mom was not particularly impressed when Jack came home with a big mark on his neck. He called it a "hickey." Mom called it disgusting. She kept asking him to invite his *young lady* over to the house so she could meet her. Jack kept coming up with excuses. He knew when Mom finally met Daphne she'd realize that she was more *lady* than *young*. Not that seventeen was old, but compared to Jack's fifteen, it was. And the fact that she was out of school and working at the plant wouldn't be in their favour either. For me, the longer this lasted, the longer I'd be left in relative peace.

It was a little strange with Jack being mostly out of the picture. Our paths hardly crossed at school, and now with him being gone in the evenings—and not wanting me to go with him—I was more on my own than I ever remembered being. When Mom was on day shift, like she was this week and next, it wasn't so bad. It was just her and me at home after supper, and I liked that. But when she went to the evening swing shift it was going to be pretty lonely around the house. Then again, that was still weeks away. She had one and a half weeks more of days, then two weeks of midnight to eight. In three and a half weeks this whole Jack and Daphne thing would probably be ancient history.

Being alone also left me with more time to think, which meant more time to imagine the kinds of things that could go wrong, all the people who could be Nazi agents or gangsters. Too much time combined with too much imagination was a bad thing.

Jack was snoring away. It was so loud it was like he was a cartoon character. The lights had been out in the living room for at least twenty minutes and I didn't hear Mom moving around now. She was probably in bed. I'd wait ten minutes more and then climb out of bed to check. I was actually feeling pretty tired, so I thought I might get to sleep pretty easily. A couple of times already I'd drifted off for a few seconds. The lack of sleep was starting to catch up with me.

Then I heard a noise. It was unmistakable—the front door opening. I rolled out of bed. I was already dressed, with my dark green canvas shoes on my feet. I wore a pyjama top in case I had to pretend to be asleep, and my dress pants because they were the only pants I had that were black. I heard the front door close again as I peeked around my bedroom door. It was being closed from the *outside*.

On all fours I crawled across the floor, getting to the window in time to see my mother walking away. Her head swivelled around. She was looking behind her and then all around, to see if anybody had seen her. I had, but she didn't know it. She headed off down the street.

I was determined to follow her, but should I wake up Jack and get him to come with me? No, there was no time for that. By the time Jack was awake and out of bed she'd be gone. Already she was disappearing into the darkness.

Quickly I ran through the house and out the back door. I closed it quietly so the sound didn't escape into the house or out into the night. I didn't want anybody to hear me. I circled around the house in time to see my mother moving down the street. She was walking on the sidewalk. There were little puddles of light cast by the scattered streetlights, and she'd appear in one of the little haloes only to disappear again into the darkness, moving toward the next one. I stayed close to the silent and sleeping houses, where there was more darkness, and where the grass and ground would muffle my footfalls. I moved quickly but not too quickly. I wanted to make sure that I didn't lose her, but I couldn't get too close or she might see me.

Almost on cue she turned her head to look and I froze in place, hidden in the shadows. She kept moving, so obviously she hadn't seen me.

For somebody who was just out for a walk she certainly seemed very nervous. Maybe that wasn't the word.

Cautious, watchful, careful. All three of those fit. I guessed walking late at night along deserted streets might explain that. Maybe not.

She turned the corner and vanished from view. I took that opportunity to cross the street and take shelter in the shadows on the other side—the side she was on. I stayed in the shadows, able to move much quicker now that she couldn't see me. Carefully I came to the last house, hugging the wall and peering around the corner. She was well down the street already, moving very quickly. This was no leisurely stroll. It was as though she was late for an appointment. But where would she be going at this time of night?

A car came rolling down the street—I hadn't noticed it at first because its lights were off. I froze, hoping the shadows would hide me. It passed and suddenly it pulled over to the curb, right in front of my mother, and I saw somebody get out! The dark figure approached my mother, and I could tell, whoever it was, he was big. Why was she still walking toward the man? Why hadn't she turned around? How could she not see him? He guided her toward the car and opened the passenger-side door and … was he forcing her into the car?

I froze in place. What was I supposed to do? Should I run to one of the houses and pound on the door and have them call the police? Why hadn't she tried to run away?

Why hadn't she screamed out or struggled? Did she know this person? And if she did, why was she out here meeting some man in the middle of the night? None of this made any sense, and from the distance I was at I couldn't really tell what was happening. I had to get closer, and fast, in case the car drove off.

I stayed close to the houses, still sure that the deep shadows would conceal me as long as I didn't move too fast. From house to house I darted, ducking behind bushes, hidden by parked cars and trees, keeping one eye on the ground in front of me and the other on the car. I could see the two dark shadows now through the back window. They were facing away from me, looking forward.

I was now close enough that if it hadn't been so dark I would have been able to read the licence plate ... was it covered with mud? I needed to get closer yet. I crawled on my belly along the grass, keeping a large bush between me and the car. I was slightly behind and to one side. To get any closer, I'd have to cross the open sidewalk, and that would put me right behind the car. On my knees I crawled across the pavement, staying so low that there was no way I could be seen in the rear-view mirror. I closed the gap and slumped down right behind the car, hidden by the trunk. I'd made it.

I took a deep breath and tried to slow down my heart, which was practically pounding through my chest.

Okay … I was here, and I could hear my mother and the big guy talking … although I couldn't hear what they were saying. My mother's voice was louder. Did that mean that her window was open? I shifted a little bit to the side. If it was open and I got a little bit closer, then I could— there was something pressed against the back of my head.

"If you move, you're dead," a foreign-sounding voice said.

CHAPTER NINE

THE BLOOD FROZE in my veins.

"No sudden movements, and raise your hands slowly above your head!" a man hissed.

As I did what I was told, my legs were kicked out from under me and I slammed, face first, into the road! A knee was pushed into the side of my head, pressing my face down so that the pavement bit painfully into my cheek.

"Don't even think about moving!"

"I … I won't," I stammered.

A second set of feet appeared and a bright light was shone into my face.

"He's just a kid!" the second voice exclaimed.

I heard the car door open and the sound of more shoes on the pavement.

"George?"

Without being able to move my head I looked up as best I could. It was Bill!

"Let my son up!"

There was my mother, standing right beside Bill! Instantly I was pulled to my feet, and my mother wrapped her arms around me.

"Everybody, into the car," Bill barked, and I was swept off my feet and practically tossed into the back seat. Bill climbed in behind the wheel and the engine roared to life. We swerved away from the curb and raced away. Headlights flashed as a second car peeled away and fell in right behind us.

"Both of you, put your heads down!" Bill ordered.

"George, your face … you're hurt!" my mother exclaimed.

I put a hand up to my face and it came away with blood on it. The side of my face had been scraped when I was thrown to the ground.

"He's hurt!" my mother yelled.

"How badly?" Bill demanded. "Do I need to get him medical help?"

"I'm okay," I said, trying to sound calm. "It's just my cheek. I'm okay … it's just a scrape!" I hoped that was all it was.

"Here," Bill said, and he passed something over the seat to my mother. It was a flashlight. She turned it on and shone it in my face. I tried to turn away but she held my head firmly and I was forced to shield my closed eyes with a hand as she examined the wound. I waited for her verdict.

"It needs to be cleaned and dressed, but it's not too bad," she finally said. "Nothing worse than you sometimes get playing road hockey."

That was a relief!

"Then that's the cover story," Bill said. "You fell while playing road hockey with your brother. That will explain it."

But that didn't explain anything else to me.

"We're clear. You can both sit up now," Bill said.

We climbed off the floor and sat on the seat.

"So, George, are you truly okay?" Bill asked.

"Oh, I'm just *great*. I'm bleeding, I was knocked to the ground, a gun was pushed into the back of my head, and I'm driving around in the back of a car in the middle of the night wondering why I'm here."

"Yes, I was wondering that myself," Bill said. "So, why are you here?"

I turned to my mother. "The better question is, why are *you* here?"

My mother didn't answer.

"Is somebody going to explain this to me? Mom?"

She looked away.

"Mom?"

She shook her head. "I can't. I'm not allowed to."

"What do you mean you're not allowed ...?"

Suddenly everything made sense. The middle of the night. Bill. Her not being "allowed" to tell me.

"That must mean that Bill is allowed," I said.

"How much do you know?" Bill asked.

Now he was asking me questions instead of answering them. Did he think I had valuable information?

"I know enough," I said.

"I'd like to hear what you know."

"Maybe *I'm* not allowed to tell *you*. Have you thought of that?" I demanded.

Bill exhaled loudly. "And how much does Jack know?"

"I guess you'd have to ask him that yourself."

"An excellent idea," he said. "Betty, I'll send a car to get Jack. Is the front door of the house open?"

"Front and back," I said. "Are you going to tell me what's happening now?"

"Sorry, George, at this point I'm not allowed to talk about it either. But I'm afraid, before the night is through, we'll have to have a discussion."

A clock ticked noisily on the shelf. I sat alone in the office—the Commander's office at Camp X. When this night started I'd had no idea where it was going to end up,

other than possibly in my bed. This was the last place ...
actually, it wasn't the last place. This all made sense. As
much sense as anything else. In a few minutes I'd have an
answer, although it might not be an answer I'd like.

I heard the door open and I spun around in time to see
Jack come in. He was wearing his housecoat and pyjamas,
slippers on his feet, his hair sticking up in a dozen different directions. I stifled a laugh. If Daphne could see him
now, that would be the end of their little romance.

"You gonna explain this to me?" he said as he staggered
over and took a seat beside me.

"I wish I could, but I don't know enough."

"You must know more than me. I'm sound asleep and I
get shoved in the side, and I wake up to three men standing over me. I practically wet myself."

This time I couldn't hold back the laughter.

"Then they tell me Bill sent them to get me," Jack said.
"I was relieved ... and then scared."

"What do you mean?"

"I noticed that you weren't in your bed. Then I found
out that you and Mom weren't in the house. I started
thinking, how do I really know that Bill sent them? How
do I know who they are?"

"Yeah, it's not like they were wearing uniforms," I
agreed, thinking back to what I'd thought when that gun
was pressed against my head.

"So I started thinking that I should make a break for it, but they were watching me like hawks, and I saw that one of them was carrying a piece under his jacket—"

"They probably all had guns," I added.

"And that made me more nervous. I wouldn't be able to run, and I was worried about where I was going and where you and Mom were."

"They didn't tell you?"

"They wouldn't tell me anything. They wouldn't say a word. That was one long car ride. I was so relieved when we drove through the front gates of the camp."

"I hope 'relieved' turns out to be the right word. I'm not sure what's going to happen. I just hope we don't have to wait too long to find out."

On cue the door opened. Mom walked in, followed by Bill and ... Little Bill! Little Bill being part of this meeting meant that we were going to get to the bottom of everything. But it also meant that this was very serious, and we'd probably stumbled into something dangerous. Again.

Mom rushed over, wrapped her arms around Jack and me. Bill brought over another chair and placed it between us, gesturing to our mother to sit down.

Little Bill stood over top of us and offered his hand. I started to get to my feet.

"Please, stay seated," he said, and I shook his hand. He did the same with Jack.

At that moment a man came into the room pushing a small serving cart. On the cart were cups and saucers, a little jug of milk, a sugar dish and a large, steaming pot of tea. I could smell it.

"Let me do the honours," Little Bill said.

He started pouring tea and then began adding milk and sugar to the cups. He handed me a cup. "Milk and three sugars," he said. "Correct?"

"Yeah."

He did the same with Bill, Jack and my mother. He didn't need to ask anybody. He had remembered from months ago how we liked our tea. Here was this man who was in charge of thousands of spies and dozens and dozens of secret operations, a man who was licensed to kill, one of the most dangerous men in the world, and he remembered how we liked our tea! Unbelievable.

"That looks like a nasty scrape," Little Bill said, pointing at my face.

"It looks worse than it is," I said, although it was still stinging. It was now partially covered by a big bandage. The medic for the camp had cleaned it out. When he'd poured the antiseptic on it, it had hurt so badly that I'd had to fight hard not to scream or cry.

"I don't believe it will leave a lasting mark, but if it does, they do say that women love a scar."

Bill and my mother laughed. I didn't think it was that funny.

"Jack, I must apologize. I'm assuming that they did not allow you sufficient time to change."

"They didn't allow me time to do anything." He pulled his housecoat a little tighter around him.

"Standard practice," he said.

"I should have mentioned to them that it would have been all right to allow him to get dressed," Bill said.

"No, it's best that they didn't deviate from established procedures. Deviation from practice can lead to disaster." He turned to us next. "So tell me, how are you boys doing in your new home?"

Jack and my mother took turns talking about the new house and school and working at the plant. I didn't say anything, I just listened. It was the strangest conversation. Here we were sitting in the middle of a top-secret spy camp, in the middle of the night, having a cup of tea and talking like we were all there for a Sunday social.

"And you, George?"

I was startled.

"How is school?" Little Bill asked.

"It's good. Fine. Okay, I guess."

"Are you managing to stay awake in class?" he asked.

"Yeah, I'm really trying hard to … how do you know about that?" I looked at my mother.

She shook her head. "I didn't tell him."

"Then how does he …?" I let the sentence trail away. I knew what he was going to say.

"We have certain connections," Little Bill said. "And you know that we have a fondness for your family and try to make sure you are all doing well."

I had no problem with them keeping an eye on us. It made me feel safer.

"So, who would like to start?" Little Bill asked.

"Don't look at me," Jack said. "I don't know nothing."

"'Anything,'" Little Bill said. "One would properly say, 'I don't know *anything*.' Good grammar is a sign of good breeding."

Jack shrugged. "Yes, sir. I don't know anything." He pointed to me. "But somehow I think this is all his fault."

"No," Little Bill said, "I believe it is *my* fault."

We gave him a questioning look.

"But let us begin closer to the beginning. George, how long have you suspected that something was, shall we say, amiss?"

"A couple of weeks, but mostly the last week."

"So you decided to follow your mother this evening."

I shrugged.

"I checked to make sure they were asleep," my mother said, "and I left as quietly as I could."

"I assume you were not, in fact, asleep, correct?" Little Bill asked.

"No."

"He's having problems getting to sleep," Jack said.

"That doesn't surprise me," Little Bill said. "That is what I assumed when I was informed that you were falling asleep in school."

"It was?" I asked.

He nodded his head. "We'll discuss that later. But first, getting back to the events of this evening, you followed your mother."

"I had to make sure she was okay. It's not safe to be out alone at night."

"You would know better than anybody of the dangers that lurk in the dark. You do worry about your mother, especially since the episode in which she was kidnapped."

"Wouldn't you?" Jack asked.

"Of course. Human nature. So you followed her because you wanted to make sure she was safe. Is that the only reason?"

"Well ... I was also pretty curious. I couldn't think of any good reason why she'd go out in the middle of the night."

"Perhaps she was just going for a walk?" Little Bill suggested.

"That's what I said!" Jack exclaimed.

"Yes, that is the logical explanation. But, of course, not the correct one."

Jack went from looking cocky to being crushed in a few brief seconds.

"So you kept your mother under surveillance as she walked."

"I was keeping an eye on her," I said.

"I didn't see him there at all," my mother said.

"And neither did our surveillance team. At least, not at first," Bill said.

"You didn't see our surveillance team either, did you?" Little Bill asked me.

"I didn't see them until the guy had a gun against my head and a knee pressed down on my temple."

Little Bill looked at Bill. "It sounds as though they executed their role very effectively."

"Quite so. Very professional. Top marks for both agents."

"George," said Little Bill, "it's important to remember when you're watching a subject that most often there will be another team assigned to watch for people watching them. You always have to have one eye on the target and a second scanning the surroundings."

"I'll try and remember that."

"I wish there had been no need for you ever to know it. So, as I understand it, you saw your mother enter Bill's car."

"I didn't know it was Bill's car," I said. "It was too dark and I was too far away. That's why I had to get closer."

"And that's when he was seen by surveillance and apprehended," Bill said.

Little Bill picked up a plate of cookies that I'd been eyeing and passed them around. I took two.

"Do you like cats, George?"

That was a strange question. "I guess I like them. We always had cats in the barn back at our farm."

"I almost see you as a cat."

"Me?"

"Yes. It's a legend that cats have nine lives, and by my count you've used up at least four and possibly five of yours."

"I guess that means I have four or five left."

Little Bill laughed. "That is certainly an interesting perspective on the situation. Would you care to hazard a guess as to why your mother was meeting with Bill?"

I didn't have any idea why … wait, yes I did! "My mother is working in the plant as an operative."

A slight smile creased Little Bill's face, and he nodded. He turned directly to Bill. "I told you the risk of employing Betty in that capacity was that the boys would discover her involvement."

"We tried to keep everything as covert as possible," Bill said.

"I am sure of that, but a good agent will smell out a plot."

"Sorry I slipped up," my mother said.

"Not your fault. For better or worse, we asked you to work as an operative, knowing that you'd have two good agents living in your house. And that is why the responsibility for this must rest with me. And now I am left with a dilemma. What do we do next?"

"Why do we have to do anything?" Jack asked. "It's not like we're going to tell anybody. We can keep a secret."

"I know you can," Little Bill said. "Please do not ever imagine that I lack complete faith in you boys. But what of other people?"

"What other people?" I asked.

"You were taken from the street two blocks from your house," he said. "Who saw your abduction? Jack was spirited out of his house in the middle of the night—was that witnessed by anybody?"

"We monitored the calls to the local constabulary," Bill said, "and there were no calls or reports to the police."

"That might only represent a false positive," Little Bill said.

Jack and I exchanged quizzical looks.

"A report would mean that you were witnessed," he explained. "No report, however, does not mean that you were not witnessed. It merely means that nothing was reported. A false positive could still be in place, and we don't know what eyes might have been on you."

"But there could have been lots of people who saw my mother get into that car," I said. "This time and other times."

"Yes, but witnessing that would only lead them to believe that your mother, a recent divorcee, was meeting a man. That would be the logical explanation. Seeing you pushed to the ground, a pistol to your head, would tend to suggest a different kind of scenario."

I hadn't thought of that.

"So, what happens now?" my mother asked, voicing the question that we were all thinking.

"It might be necessary to relocate you again."

"But I don't want to move!" Jack exclaimed. "I like it here!"

I knew what he was thinking. Actually, I knew *who* he was thinking of.

"Nevertheless ...," Little Bill began.

"That isn't fair," Jack went on. "If *somebody* had kept his nose out of other people's business, none of this would have happened."

I couldn't look at my brother. I felt my whole body flush.

"I am afraid that if blame is to be placed, it must be placed squarely on my shoulders," Little Bill said again. "I hope you can find it in your heart to forgive me, Jack."

"Forgive you?"

"Yes. I should have allowed you all, the whole family, to keep a safe distance from further operations. I am truly sorry. Now, if you can excuse me, prior to making my decision I need to think and consult. Could you go and wait in the outer office?"

We all stood up.

"All of you except for George."

I froze in my tracks. "Me?"

He nodded his head and pointed. "Yes, you."

CHAPTER TEN

EVERYBODY, INCLUDING BILL, shuffled out of the room. My mother gave me a very worried look as she left, and her face was the last thing I saw as Bill slowly closed the door behind them.

Little Bill pulled a chair over until he was sitting directly across from me, and very close. I drew slightly away, pressing against the back of my chair, the hairs on the back of my neck standing on end.

"Don't be nervous, George. You've done nothing wrong."

I appreciated the words, but if I hadn't done anything wrong, why was I still here?

"You're probably not aware of this, George, but you are, without a doubt, the finest twelve-year-old spy in the entire world."

"I am?"

"Unquestionably. Not simply because there are not many twelve-year-old spies, but because there are very few people, even trained agents, who have your feel for this business. Some think of it as almost an art."

"Like painting?"

"Well, there is a very strong creative component. Depending on the kind of work involved, you might think of it as the art of deception, of thinking quickly and critically, or of making up stories and lies, and, in some extremes, as the art of killing."

I'd seen people killed. There was no art involved, as far as I could tell.

"Have you ever heard the term 'shell shock'?" Little Bill asked.

I shook my head.

"It was first used in World War I."

"You served in that war, right?"

"First in the trenches. My infantry career was ended with a poison gas attack. Almost killed me. I was evacuated to London and placed in the hospital. Life and death, really—my lungs were so damaged that they told me there was no way I could fight in the trenches any more."

"So the war was over for you."

"That's exactly what the doctor said to me. I told him that since the war wasn't over, it wasn't over for me. I informed him that if I couldn't fight in the trenches then

I would learn how to fight above them. That's when I became a pilot."

"That must have been exciting."

"It was. It was remarkably easy to become a pilot in those days since pilots survived only two weeks on average, so they were always looking for new ones ... but that's a story for another time. In that war, one would often soften up a target by throwing hundreds and sometimes thousands of artillery shells at the enemy position."

"Like the ammunition that they make at the plant?"

"Almost identical. Sitting in the trenches, you could hear the shells as they came flying through the air. It was a strange sound, almost musical, like a whistle. And in time you got to know when and how close they were going to land. If it was a direct hit you were dead, so there really wasn't much to worry about. A close hit could spray you with shrapnel, shell fragments. A number of times I was hit by mud—for an instant you'd think it was shrapnel, and then you'd realize it was nothing but a mud bath. Either way, all you could do was sit in the trench and wait and pray that you wouldn't be hit."

"That must have been awful."

He nodded. "Beyond belief. As soldiers we were often forced to stay in those trenches for extended periods, living through repeated artillery barrages. It was hard on all, but for some it was too much. They suffered from what we called 'shell shock.' They seemed to break down mentally to the point that they couldn't function. Some would become catatonic."

"What does that mean?"

"They would just sit there, eyes open, staring, not answering questions, or seeming to hear what was being said to them. Others would get up and run away. Still stranger, others would become so fearless that they would stand up so that they were exposed to enemy fire, even charge toward that fire. In all cases they were no longer fit to fight, they were 'shell shocked.' It was believed that somehow the sound and vibration of the shells had addled their minds. We now tend to call it 'battle fatigue.' Men who have been in too many battles need to be taken out of the front lines and given rest to prevent them from becoming shell shocked."

"That makes sense."

"Yes, it does. George, do you think you're feeling shell shocked, feeling battle fatigue?"

"Me? I've never been in battle!" I protested.

He reached out and put a hand on my shoulder. "Yes, you have. You have been in many life-and-death battles."

"I'm okay."

"Some of the symptoms of battle fatigue include not being able to sleep, feeling worried or anxious all the time, not being able to concentrate. George, can you honestly say that you haven't been feeling all of those?"

I shook my head ever so slightly. "I've always been sort of nervous about things. That doesn't mean that ..." I let the sentence trail off because I knew what he was going to say. He was going to move us again. He was going to pull my mother out of the plant and off of her mission and give me a chance to rest.

"You can't do it," I said.

"I can't do what?"

"You can't make us leave."

"George, there may not be any choice."

"Yes there is. Can I ask you a question?"

"Of course," Little Bill answered.

"You wouldn't have asked my mother to work as an operative at the plant unless something very important was happening there, right?"

"You can assume that it has a high level of importance."

"That whole plant is important," I said. "I know that. I also know that it's one of the biggest potential targets the Nazis would want to destroy."

"Also correct."

"Without ammunition the men can't fight. Without ammunition my father can't fight. If having to make my mother move would jeopardize the defence of the factory, then that would put our soldiers at risk ... it would put my father at risk."

"We cannot win the war without the tools to fight," Little Bill agreed.

"And finally, the fact that you're hesitating to pull my mother away means that something big is about to happen really soon. You know that the plant is at risk ... and you don't have time to replace her."

He didn't answer.

"Right?"

"You are basing these assumptions on an almost complete absence of information."

"But I'm right ... aren't I?"

"I was wrong when I said you were probably the best twelve-year-old operative in the world."

That could only mean that I was wrong. I felt myself deflate.

"You might be," he continued, "one of the best operatives around of *any* age."

I felt a wave of relief wash over me ... or should I be relieved? Did that mean the plant was at risk ... that my mother was at risk because of that?

"Then I'm right?"

He nodded his head ever so slightly. "May I inquire as to how you came to this conclusion?"

"I know how important the plant is and I figured that you wouldn't have put my mother in there if you didn't really need her, because you really didn't want me or Jack around any more dangerous things because you wondered if we were shelled."

He laughed. "Shell *shocked*. But, obviously, not enough to cloud your judgment or your thought processes. My congratulations, sir," he said, and he offered his hand.

"So that means that we can stay and help?" I asked.

"That decision has yet to be made."

"But if you pulled my mother out right now it could endanger the defence of the plant, so you can't do that. You have to let her finish her mission."

"What if that mission places her and you and your brother at increased risk?" Little Bill said.

"You should tell us the risks and let us make the decision. But I'm telling you right now, if it's important, then we have to stay. We *all* have to stay. My mother is going to finish her job and we're going to stay here to help her, and that's all there is to it."

His dark eyes glared brightly for a second and I felt a wave of anxiety wash over me.

"No disrespect, sir," I added.

"None taken. And how do you feel that you and your brother could help?"

"I'm not exactly sure, but I think we could do something. Mr. Granger thinks we could be helpful, you know, as two more pairs of eyes on the place."

"I'm aware of Mr. Granger's position."

"You are?"

"Yes. He contacted me last week asking that very same thing. Of course I turned him down."

He stopped talking, but I could tell that he was still thinking. He was mulling over the choices. I had to give him more help in deciding.

"That plant is important," I said. "For our side to win, for men like my father to fight, they need the weapons and ammunition to do the job. We can't let anybody stop them from doing their jobs. I do need to rest, but not now. After this is over you can move us someplace quiet and I promise I won't ever be curious about anything again."

Little Bill burst into laughter. "I'm afraid you ceasing to be curious is not a possibility. It is part of who you are." He paused. "Do you trust me, George?"

"Yeah, of course!"

"Good, because you are going to have to trust that my decision is best. Now go and join your mother and brother. I'll arrange to have you all driven home."

"But what about the decision?"

"That will require time and consideration. After all, something very important is at stake here ... the very lives of the members of your family."

CHAPTER ELEVEN

THERE WAS A KNOCK on the classroom door and I started slightly. I wasn't asleep, I'd been thinking hard about the math problem on the board. I hadn't slept more than two hours the night before but I wasn't sleepy. Instead my mind seemed incredibly sharp and focused. The only way I could keep the events of last night out of my head—the only way to stop thinking about what my talk with Little Bill might soon lead to—was to follow the lessons as if my life depended on them.

My teacher took a note from the kid at the door, opened it up and glanced down at it.

"George," she called out. "You are requested at the office ... again."

There were the usual *ooohs* from the other kids. I was surprised too. What could this be about? I hadn't fallen asleep in class lately, and I'd been on time every day. Both my watch and I had been keeping good time.

"Don't look so worried," my teacher said, with a smile.

"Thanks," I mumbled, although that seemed like a pretty stupid thing to say. I put my pencil down and walked out of the class into the empty hallway.

My teacher had it wrong. I was surprised, but I wasn't worried. There was nothing a principal could do to me that would make me worry. Last night I'd had a gun pressed against my head—again—and been thrown to the pavement and practically scared to death. No matter what, I was pretty sure the principal wasn't armed ... well, except for the strap. He had his hanging from a nail on the wall where everybody could see it when they were called into his office. Suddenly I did feel a tiny bit worried.

The way things were looking, though, I figured there was probably a fifty-fifty chance that my days at this school were numbered. We'd probably be moved and start at another school, maybe far away. At least then Jack could be his own age again. He'd like that. He wouldn't like leaving Daphne behind, though, and if that had to happen he was going to make my life miserable—and at least a little painful. As far as Jack was concerned this was all my fault, and he had certainly let me know that last night when I'd told him what Little Bill had said to me about shell shock.

I entered the outer office—the secretary was nowhere to be seen. Should I sit down and wait, or knock on the principal's door or—?

"What trouble have you got us in now?"

I turned around. It was Jack.

"I didn't get us in any trouble," I said. "I must be here because of something *you* did."

"The only mistake I made was having a little brother who—"

"Gentlemen."

It was Mr. McGregor, standing at the door to his office. He stood tall, his back perfectly straight, no hint of emotion on his face, although his thick, bushy moustache twitched slightly. Funny, there was something about him that reminded me of Little Bill. Maybe it was his attitude of being in charge.

He motioned for us to enter his office, and we went directly to the two seats in front of his desk. I was about to sit down until Jack reached over and gave me a tap on the arm to remind me not to take a seat until we had been given permission.

Mr. McGregor circled around his desk and took a seat.

"Please be seated."

We settled into the two chairs.

"You are probably wondering why you were called down here," he began.

"Yes, sir," Jack said.

"Well, so am I," Mr. McGregor said.

"What?" I said, without thinking. "I mean, what, *sir*?"

"And most likely I won't be told," he continued, which only added to my confusion.

"Would you like me to leave?" he asked.

"No, I think you should remain," came a voice from behind us.

My head spun around. It was Bill! I jumped to my feet. It was as if he'd materialized out of thin air, like a rabbit pulled from a hat, but there was no hat. He was sitting in a chair, right behind the door, partially blocked from view by a coat rack.

Bill strolled over and slapped both of us on the back. "You should always look around a room when you enter. Haven't I taught you two boys anything?" He perched himself on the edge of the principal's desk.

"Are you sure I should stay?" Mr. McGregor asked.

"I imagine it would be hard to explain the two boys being in your office if you were seen elsewhere. How long will it be before your secretary returns?"

"She'll be gone for at least forty minutes."

"Excellent.

"As you boys must now realize, Mr. McGregor is one of our operatives.

"Did either of you suspect?" he asked us.

"No, sir."

"No way," Jack said.

"Mr. McGregor has served our government in two wars and in the peace between them," Bill said.

"It was my duty," he said. "And now I serve here as a principal."

"And as our operative," Bill added.

"So you knew all about us, right?" Jack asked.

"Everything I needed to know to help keep you safe."

"Safe from what?" I questioned.

"From whatever might evolve," Bill said. "We hoped that your cover would provide a level of safety, but, as always, we like to have a backup. That would be Mr. McGregor."

"I've had at least one eye on you two boys the whole time you've been here," he said. "If intervention had been necessary, then ..." He undid the top button of his suit jacket and pulled it open to reveal a pistol in a holster tucked away where it wouldn't be seen.

"Mr. McGregor is one of the best shots I've ever met."

"You are too generous."

They continued to talk, and I tried to figure out if it was good or bad that this was happening in front of Mr. McGregor. Did that mean that it didn't matter, because we were leaving the school, leaving town? Or was he involved because he had to know more since we were staying?

"Now, back to the purpose of our meeting," Bill said.

"So, do we go or stay?" Jack asked abruptly.

"You're going to stay," Bill said.

Jack's face beamed. I felt relieved, but also concerned.

"For now," Bill added.

Jack's smile quickly faded.

"And will everything stay the same?" I asked.

Jack gave me a confused look.

"I mean, will we stay on the sidelines, or are we going to be doing something more than just going to school?" I asked.

A small smile came to Bill's face. "Little Bill told me what you said last night, about how important the work we do is. And, well, we need both of you again." He turned to Jack. "Are you in?"

"Of course I'm in!"

"So, what are we going to be doing?" I asked.

"Tomorrow, Mr. McGregor will be announcing a writing contest," Bill said. "Students will have five days to explain, in writing, why they think they would be a good newspaper reporter. Do you still think you'd like to be a reporter?" Bill asked me.

"Sure, yeah, of course."

"Excellent, because you are going to *win* the contest."

"I always knew the boy had talent!" Mr. McGregor laughed.

"And as your prize for winning the contest, you will become a regular contributor to the plant newsletter, *The Commando*. You'll be writing a weekly column called 'A Kid's Eye View.' As a reporter, you will be authorized to be on the grounds of the plant ... and can wander almost anywhere you want."

I understood. "But I don't know if I can write a column every week."

"Every second week or so will be fine. We will also be able to use your column to pass messages to our operatives within the plant."

"You mean using a secret code, like 'Ireland'?" Ireland was a code in which the first letters of all the words in a sentence were put together to form the real message.

"I'm afraid that might be too easily interpreted by anyone looking for a coded message. Instead, we'll ask you to insert certain key words or phrases into your report," Bill said. "That way, we won't have to risk any more direct contact with our operatives in the plant, like the meeting that allowed you to break your mother's cover."

"You said 'operatives,' plural," I began, "so there must be more than just my mother."

"There are many."

"And you must suspect that there are bad guys working there as well," I added.

"We have our suspicions, but insufficient proof to aim a finger at anybody in particular. Now, it is important that all communications between you two and Camp X go through Mr. McGregor."

"May I suggest," Mr. McGregor said, "that if there is a need for the boys to pass on information they simply do something that will result in a visit to the office?"

"You mean … do something bad? On *purpose*?" Jack asked.

"Exactly, although I wouldn't recommend doing anything *too* wrong," Mr. McGregor said. He gestured to the strap hanging on the wall. "If you did something that would normally result in a student receiving the strap, then I would have to give you the strap to keep your cover intact."

"You're kidding, right?"

Mr. McGregor shook his head. "Can't have you being involved in fisticuffs and not receiving a good strapping. Now that wouldn't seem fair or reasonable, would it?"

I felt my palms getting sweaty as I eyed the thick leather strap hanging there.

"Maybe you should leave it to us to figure out what needs to be done to get down here," Jack said. "But I'm still not sure what I'm going to be doing while George is playing newspaper reporter."

"Ah, yes," Bill said. "I'm afraid you'll soon be coming down here again to see Mr. McGregor. You're going to be expelled."

"What?" Jack exclaimed.

"Yes. We need an explanation to justify you leaving school."

"But ... but ..." Jack was almost speechless—a very rare occurrence.

"It's necessary for you to leave school in order for you to begin your employment at the plant. You'll begin working there before the end of the week."

"I'm going to work at the plant!"

"Yes. Maintenance Department. That will give you free access to the entire facility, which is essential if we are to fully utilize your observational skills."

That made perfect sense. Both Jack and I would be free to wander around the plant. Jack could report things to me and I could report them to Mr. McGregor, who would get the information back to Bill and Little Bill.

"Wait a minute," Jack said. "Let me get this straight—my mother agreed to let me get expelled from school? She didn't *mind*?"

"Well, to suggest that she didn't mind might be going too far, but yes, she did agree, on the understanding that this would be a short-term arrangement only. As George has already deduced, we anticipate that any action against the plant will happen sooner rather than later. You'll be back at school before too long, Jack—if not here, then somewhere else. And if you need any extra tutoring because of classes missed, we'll do what we can to help."

"Oh, thanks," Jack said, somewhat sarcastically, I thought. "Thanks a *lot!*"

"Now, if there are no further questions, I suggest that you two boys return to class. I'll make my own exit before your secretary returns," Bill said.

We both stood up, and Bill and then Mr. McGregor offered us their hands.

"It's a pleasure to be working with you boys once again," Bill said.

"Thanks," I mumbled.

"Now both of you, back to class."

When we left, the outer office was still empty; the secretary hadn't returned.

"Somehow this doesn't seem fair," Jack said.

"What do you mean?"

"First off, you got to keep your name and keep your grade. Me, I had to be John and I had to fail a grade."

"Well, that's all going to end now, at least."

"Yeah, you get to win a contest and I get to be expelled! How's that for fair?"

"On the bright side, you get to spend more time with Daphne," I said.

"That *is* a bright side," he agreed as he burst into a big smile.

"And you won't have to lie about what grade you're in because you'll be working at the factory, too," I added.

"Again correct. And there's one more good thing about this," Jack said.

"What's that?"

"I get to choose how I'm going to get expelled."

"What do you have in mind?" I asked.

Jack smiled. "You'll have to wait ... at least until lunch."

"Lunch ... today?"

"In a few minutes. No time to waste. If you want to watch, be there in the yard."

"Jack ... you're not going to do anything stupid, are you?"

"Of course I'm going to do something stupid. If I don't, I won't get expelled. See you in a few minutes."

I choked down my lunch, watching the clock, waiting for the bell to sound and release us so we could go out to the yard. I really wasn't very hungry. The second hand swept around. All I wanted to do was get out there and——the bell rang out at last, and everyone scurried to leave the classroom. I stuffed my lunch bag into my desk and jumped to my feet. Whatever Jack had in mind, I had no intention of missing it.

I was one of the first out, and I watched as other kids started to spill out into the yard. I didn't care about anybody else except Jack. The high school kids came out through the middle double doors—the ones I was standing right in front of.

What sorts of things could you do that would get you expelled? Defying a teacher ... breaking something ... a fight ... or would that only get you the strap, or suspended?

Jack came out through the doors. He saw me, smiled and gave me a little wave. He looked amused, as though he had a really good secret or a story or a joke that he knew but nobody else did, and soon, he was going to share it.

I started to move toward him but he shook his head. I stopped in my tracks. Jack started walking away from the kids on the pavement and over to the large tree in the yard. Standing under the tree were the oldest kids, the grade thirteen students. There were a dozen of them, mostly girls. A lot of the boys in grade thirteen had turned eighteen already, dropped out of school and enlisted.

Jack stopped right in front of the group. They didn't seem to notice him standing there. I went closer, but stayed a safe distance away.

"Hey, ugly!" Jack yelled out.

Everybody turned around and looked at him. A lot of the playground noise stopped.

"You sure are ugly!" Jack said loudly.

Again there was no answer from anybody.

"Are you deaf as well as ugly?" Jack asked now.

"You talking to me?" It was Brad.

"You're the one who answered, so you must think you're ugly, too!" Jack snapped.

He stepped forward menacingly. I knew Brad the way every kid in the school knew him. He was big—a lot bigger than Jack—and he was a bully. He was always shooting off his mouth and picking on somebody, sometimes kids who were a whole lot younger. I'd seen him take a football from a kid in grade four and kick it over the fence into the woods. The kid burst into tears, and Brad laughed at him.

"You looking for a fight?" Brad demanded.

"If I was, I wouldn't be talking to you," Jack said.

"You better not be."

"Yeah, 'cause I've been watching, and it looks like you only fight little kids. You wouldn't want to mess with somebody as big as me."

"You're not that big," Brad snarled.

"But you are that *ugly*," Jack said.

There was a ripple of laughter from the crowd that had started to circle around the two of them.

"I'm tired of you acting like you're a big man, picking on little kids," Jack said. "Come on, try picking on somebody your own size."

"Nobody here *is* my size," Brad boasted.

"Then I guess I'll have to cut you down to *my* size."

"You're going to regret ever messing with me," Brad snarled.

"The only thing I regret is not kicking the crap out of you the first time I saw that ugly face."

More and more kids were joining the crowd now. I had to struggle to make sure I maintained my spot in the front. As they were talking, Jack and Brad were slowly circling around each other. I knew Jack could fight, but this guy was big—*really* big.

"So you gonna dance or are you going to fight?" Jack demanded. "Because you're so ugly this is the only dance you're going to get."

"Shut up!" Brad yelled.

"Maybe you should *make* me shut up. Just pretend I'm only ten years old ... pretend I'm a girl ... no way ... *you're* the little girl ... a stupid, ugly, little—"

"Aaahhhh!" Brad screamed as he rushed at Jack.

Jack sidestepped and then stuck out his foot. Brad tripped over it and crashed to the ground with a thunderous thud! He jumped to his feet and spun around and that's when Jack smashed him right in the face! There was a gasp from the crowd, and Brad tumbled over backwards, hitting the ground like a fallen tree! His hands were clasped over his face, and there was blood, lots of blood, flowing around his fingers.

"Break it up!" came a voice from behind.

It was Mr. McGregor. He moved forward and the crowd parted for him like Moses at the Red Sea, letting him through. He looked at Jack and then looked down at Brad, who was still on the ground but was now sitting up. Blood was dripping down his shirt and his nose looked like it was at a strange angle.

"What is the meaning of this?" Mr. McGregor demanded. "This is a school, not a jungle. There is to be no fighting in my school."

"It wasn't much of a fight," Jack snarled.

Mr. McGregor's expression turned to icy anger. "Both of you into my office, immediately!"

Brad tried to get to his feet, but he staggered and sagged back down to the ground. Jack had really put a pasting on him.

"You!" he yelled at Jack. "Help him to his feet."

Jack shook his head. "I helped him down. Somebody else can help him up." I couldn't believe that Jack was defying the principal ... wait, that was what he was supposed to be doing.

"That is an order!" Mr. McGregor yelled. "You are already facing a suspension. If you do not do as you are ordered then it will be an expulsion!"

"Don't waste your breath, old man. I've got better places to be than here. I'll consider myself expelled!"

Jack stomped away, brushing first past Mr. McGregor and then Brad. He walked right toward where I stood and the rest of the crowd stepped aside, making way for him to pass. He nodded at me and then gave me a little wink as he walked away. I turned and watched—everybody in the entire school watched—as he walked across the yard, through the gate and disappeared down the street.

Wow ... I had to give him credit. It had taken him less than an hour to get expelled, and he'd done it in a way that nobody there would ever forget. Especially not Brad.

CHAPTER TWELVE

I SEARCHED the typewriter keys looking for the letter *q*. It didn't seem to be there … okay, there it was, hiding in plain sight above the *a* key. I pushed it down. Using a typewriter seemed to be the hardest part of my new job. Finding something to write about was easy. Typing it up was hard. Now I had even more admiration for those secretaries down in the plant offices. They could type like there was no tomorrow. They didn't even have to look at the keys. It was amazing.

"So, here it is!" It was Mr. Chalmers, the editor of *The Commando* and my boss. "Hot off the press. And you're on page one." He slapped a copy of the newsletter down on the desk.

There it was, just below the fold of the paper, and the headline read, "Helping My Father Fight the Nazis!"

"I didn't expect it to be on the front page," I said.

"And I didn't expect it to be so good."

"Thanks."

"Especially after that first article you wrote," he added.

"You didn't like it?" I asked, feeling both surprised and hurt.

"Not particularly."

My first article had been introducing myself and explaining that I was going to be writing a regular column in the newsletter.

"But I have to be honest," he said, "I wasn't crazy about this whole idea to begin with. Matter of fact, I told them it was downright stupid ... not to mention insulting."

"Insulting?"

"Yeah. Every darn fool who can hold a pen and knows the alphabet thinks he can write. Here I am trying to put out a professional publication, and they think that any school kid can help write it."

"I'm sorry ... I didn't mean to—"

"It's not you, kid," he said, cutting me off. "You've been nothing but respectful. I think you could make a fine reporter one day."

"That's what I'm hoping for," I said.

He looked surprised. "You are?"

"Yes, sir. Telling the truth is one of the best ways to support democracy and fight Fascism."

Now he looked even more surprised. "I couldn't have said it better myself."

"I know that one of the first things Hitler did was shut down the newspapers," I added. "He was afraid of the truth, and that's what a newspaper report is there to do, report the truth."

"When I hear you talking like that, it's no wonder you won that contest."

"Thanks," I mumbled. I still felt a little guilty because I knew the contest had been fixed. If William Shakespeare had entered an essay he would have finished second to me.

"I'd really like to see the story you wrote to win the contest."

So would I, I thought. Over seventy students had written entries, but I wasn't one of them.

"I think my principal, Mr. McGregor, has it."

"Perhaps you can get it from him."

"I'll try to remember to ask."

"This story is exactly what we need to write," Mr. Chalmers said, as he tapped a finger against the article. "Letting people know who your father is. You must be very proud of him."

"I am." Although, the father I wrote about in the article was a pilot in Europe, not a soldier in Africa—all part of keeping my cover intact. So much for my big talk about "the truth." I guess it was like Little Bill said, "Truth is the first casualty of war."

"One of the missions of this newspaper is to use truth to build morale and increase production. You talked about your father, but what you were doing was reminding people that our fighting men are people's fathers and brothers and husbands. And by working harder on the line, taking pride in the ammunition they're making, they're keeping our fighting men safe and helping to win the war."

"Thanks."

"So how long have you wanted to be a reporter?"

"Since I was young."

He laughed. "As opposed to the old man you are now?"

"Well …"

"Nothing wrong with being young … although it's so long ago that I was young that I can hardly remember."

"You're not that old," I said.

"You're not that good a liar. If I wasn't old I'd be over there fighting instead of here writing about the fighting."

"Everybody is fighting in a different way," I said. "You're doing your part by writing the newspaper and driving up production."

He smiled. "Speaking of which, I think it's time for me to go out and do my part. I'm going off-site to do an interview. Pull the door closed when you leave the office."

"Yes, sir. I'm going in a minute myself, to have lunch at the cafeteria. Maybe I can eat with my brother ... he's working today."

He looked at his watch. "It's twenty to twelve."

"I'd better get going, I lost track of the time."

"That happens to me when I'm in the middle of a story. You'd better hurry out."

The cafeteria was in one of the buildings in the middle of the grounds, and our office was on the far side—a good distance away.

"Why don't you take the camera with you?" Mr. Chalmers suggested.

"But ... I'm just going to lunch."

"There's no telling when a story might come your way. Besides, it's not doing any good sitting on the counter in the corner. Go ahead, take it."

I took the camera and we left the office together. He pulled the door closed, revealing the lettering on the glass: "*THE COMMANDO*: A VOICE FOR DEMOCRACY."

"I won't be back until tomorrow," Mr. Chalmers said. "Are you going to be around?"

"Definitely."

"You know, this isn't supposed to be a full-time job for you."

"My mother and brother are both working tomorrow,

so I've got nothing else to do, really. What else is there to do on a Sunday?"

"I guess I'll see you, then."

Mr. Chalmers went off to his car and I headed for the cafeteria. I had just enough time to get there—actually, if I timed things right I might get there early. Since the plant was so large and spread out there was a big, old bus that went from building to building. But there was no one waiting at the bus stop—I must have missed it. I'd have to walk.

Mr. Chalmers was right, I was spending all the time I could around the plant. That was partly because I knew the more I was there, the better the chances of finding out something. It was a pretty fascinating place, and I'd got to know it well over the last two weeks.

The whole grounds took up almost three thousand acres, and there were more than a hundred buildings and outbuildings on it. The plant was deliberately designed so that the buildings were spread out. That way, a fire would be less likely to spread, and any explosion would be more isolated. A lot of the buildings—more than half of them—had banks of earth heaped up around them. That meant that there was something explosive or flammable inside. If there were an explosion, then the barriers would direct the force of the blast up instead of out.

Over the past three months there had been a drive at the plant to increase production by twenty-five percent, so a whole lot of people had been hired—over a thousand new employees. There were now ten thousand workers. Because they worked on three shifts, seven days a week, at any given time almost one-third of them were in the plant. Almost another third weren't working but were still on the grounds. Many of the unmarried employees— people like Daphne—lived right there. There were buildings, Women's Residences, each of which held one hundred women. There were five different buildings like that for women and one for men. And employees stuck around for the social activities, too—movies twice a week, bingo once a week, Saturday evening dances.

One thing I'd been checking out was the procedure at the front gates as people came into the plant. The guards there tried their best, but they really didn't have the manpower to inspect everybody thoroughly. There was also a time factor. They couldn't delay people at the gate or the line wouldn't start on time. They needed to let people through to keep production up. But they could have been letting anybody through, carrying anything. I knew a little bit about plastic explosives. Somebody could bring in a piece the size of a slice of bread—heck, it could be smuggled into the plant in somebody's sandwich—and nobody would ever know. Not until they'd smuggled in enough to blow up the whole plant. That didn't make me feel very secure.

I made it to the cafeteria and stepped inside. It was a bustle of activity. This was where the people who lived on the grounds ate all their meals, while a lot of shift workers would often come here, even if they'd brought their own food.

Hundreds of people were waiting in line, trays in hand, and it seemed as though every seat at every one of the dozens and dozens of tables was filled. The workers were mainly women. Some were older, my mother's age, and then there were those like Daphne who should have still been in school. Almost all of them had their hair pinned up and held in place by kerchiefs and bandanas.

Jack was spending a lot of time with Daphne—not only breaks and lunch, but most evenings. He'd somehow arranged for the two of them to have the same shift—a different shift from my mother's. This meant that my mother didn't know how much time they were spending together, though I was pretty sure she suspected. I didn't care about that. What bugged me was that Jack was spending too much time looking at Daphne and not enough time looking around. It was hard to see spies when you had stars in your eyes.

I walked through the cafeteria, looking from table to table, from face to face, trying to find him. There were a few men, but no Jack. He was in the Maintenance Department, so his breaks could be different from everybody else's. I knew he'd want to be here now, though, because Daphne was going to have her lunch break. I didn't see her, either.

Just then Doris and Juliette came strolling in with a bunch of other girls—none of them were Daphne, but they might know where she was. If I found her, I'd probably find Jack.

I went over. "Hello!"

"Hi, Georgie!" Juliette sang out.

"I was wondering if you've seen my brother."

"He's outside at the picnic table with Daphne."

"Good, I'm going to—"

"Haven't you heard the expression *two's company, three's a crowd*?" Juliette said. She reached out and took my arm. "Unless you want to make it a double date?"

"Like I told you before, you're not mature enough for me." I brushed her hand off and walked away.

"Does this mean we're over?" Juliette called out after me.

I didn't turn around. I kept walking. If she wanted to look like a fool that was her business.

Outside, I saw them almost immediately. They were sitting side by side, by themselves, at a picnic table, in the shade cast by one of the buildings. I walked right up to them. They were so absorbed, staring at each other, that they didn't notice me practically standing right on top of them. So much for Jack keeping his eyes open.

Finally he looked up. He didn't look pleased to see me.

"Hello, George," Daphne said sweetly. She didn't seem unhappy. "Do you want to join us?" she asked.

"No, he doesn't!" Jack said.

I ignored my brother and sat down on the empty side opposite them. Jack went from not pleased to really angry in the blink of an eye. I didn't care. I had the trump card, because I knew things that he didn't want either Daphne or Mom to know.

"My guess is that he misses you," Daphne said to Jack. "I know *I* would." She reached over and took his hand and his whole face softened.

"I do miss him," I agreed, and I wasn't lying about that. Between my school and his shifts I hadn't seen him in days.

"So, how's school going?" Jack asked.

"About the same."

"And how is my buddy's eye looking these days?"

"A little bit better. It's more purple than black."

"What's with the camera?" Jack asked.

"Mr. Chalmers wants me to get to know how to use it so I can publish pictures with my column sometimes."

"Take a picture of us," Daphne said. She slid in closer to Jack.

I brought the camera up to my eye and tried to focus it. It was a pretty complicated camera and I wasn't really sure how to use it.

"You gonna take that picture or what?" Jack asked.

"I'm trying to get it right," I said. "After all, Mom will want to at least see what Daphne looks like."

Jack's face looked like thunder.

"I'd like to meet her, too," Daphne said. "It's just that we don't ever seem to find a time that works."

"That was a very good article you wrote," Jack said.

I knew what he was doing. He was trying to change the subject.

"It was very good," Daphne agreed. "Everybody on my line was talking about it. I told them it was written about my boyfriend's father by his brother."

Jack beamed—I think it was the *boyfriend* comment, and not because he was proud of my writing.

A short ways off from where we sat, the big employee bus rumbled up and came to a stop. I looked at it and then did a double take—there was thick black smoke coming from under the hood. It looked like it was overheating or—everybody was rushing off the bus, screaming and yelling! It wasn't overheating. The bus was on fire!

CHAPTER THIRTEEN

JACK AND I both jumped up from the bench and ran closer. The driver, who was really old, had scrambled off the bus and was desperately trying to open the hood. The heat and the smoke drove him back, but he tried over and over again. He pulled off his jacket and wrapped it around one hand to protect him from the heat as he struggled to pop the latch. When the hood opened he was practically thrown backwards by the flames. He started to scream in pain—he must have been burned!

Thick black smoke and bright orange flames soared upward. Despite it all, the engine of the bus was somehow still running. People gathered around to watch, and then I remembered that I still had the camera. I didn't need to just watch, I could take pictures. I pulled the camera up and took a few—

"What are you doing?" Jack demanded.

"I'm trying to—"

"That bus … it can't stay here … it might explode."

Jack broke through the crowd and ran for the bus. For a split second I stood frozen in place.

"Here, take this," I said to Daphne, and handed her the camera.

I went after Jack, who ran through the open door of the bus and up the stairs, jumping into the driver's seat. This time I didn't hesitate. I jumped on as he clanked the bus into gear and it started to move!

"Get off!" Jack yelled.

"No!" I screamed.

"It might blow up! I have to get it away from the buildings!"

He inched the bus forward and started to crank the wheel to go left. I reached out and turned it the other way.

"No, no! To the right, the best way is to go right!"

"Are you sure?"

"Left takes you closer to more buildings! Just do what I'm telling you!"

He cranked the wheel to the right and the bus groaned as it made the turn.

Jack craned his neck to try to see forward, around the raised hood and through the smoke and the flames. He could hardly see anything so he couldn't move any faster, but he couldn't afford not to go faster.

I climbed down the steps, grabbed the railing and leaned out through the open door. That way I could see around and in front.

"To the right!" I yelled. "Turn to the right!"

Jack did what I ordered and he curved around a building, but a second one appeared right in front of us.

"Now left ... left ... left!" I screamed.

He cranked the wheel and the bus jerked and I was flung around, my strong grip on the railing the only thing that stopped me from flying right out the open door. I regained my balance and tried to peer through the smoke and flame.

"Straight, and go faster!" I yelled.

Jack changed gears and there was a loud grinding sound. The bus momentarily slowed and then jumped forward as the engine raced. We were coming up quickly to an embankment and would have to turn fast.

"Get ready to hang another right!" I yelled.

"Just tell me when."

"Soon ... in about five seconds ... four ... three ... two ... now! Turn the wheel hard!"

The whole bus tilted as Jack cranked the wheel, and this time the force sent me flying back into the bus. I tried to hang on but we seemed to be up on two wheels and I thought that we were going to tip over! The bus slammed sideways into the embankment and we bounced back, almost tipping the other way before it regained its balance and we rocketed forward with all four wheels on the ground.

"What now?" Jack yelled.

I scrambled down the stairs again, trying to move fast but afraid of the ground that was passing by even more quickly below the open door. I grabbed the rail and leaned out, but the smoke was thicker and the flames were higher. I couldn't see anything.

"George, what do I do?" Jack yelled. There was desperation in his voice.

I went to the bottom step, still clinging to the rail. I leaned around the open door and I was hit in the face by wind and smoke and heat. I used my free hand to partially block my eyes and then looked forward and—we were coming up quickly to another building!

"Brake! Brake! Brake!" I screamed.

The words had barely escaped my lips when Jack slammed on the brakes. The bus slowed dramatically, but I didn't! My face smashed into the door. Pain shot up into my brain, and I nearly lost my grip on the railing.

I recovered my scrambled senses quickly. "Crank it to the left!" I screamed.

The bus groaned as it swerved and made the turn and—the windshield cracked and then shattered, showering pieces of glass into the bus! There was a surge of heat and the smoke flowed into the vehicle! I looked over at Jack—he was crouched down in the seat, desperately trying to use the dashboard as protection.

There was no time to think—no time to be cautious. I leaned out and tried to see the next turn. Ahead, through the smoke, I could see only green field. We raced by the last building. We were past the buildings, we were safe ... no, we were still in danger ... we had to get off the bus!

"Jack, it's okay, stop the bus, we're past the buildings!"

"Get off!" Jack yelled. "Jump!"

"What?"

"Jump!"

"We're going too fast!" I screamed.

Jack hit the brakes hard and the bus slowed—although you wouldn't have guessed it looking at the ground hurtling by outside the door.

"Jump! I'll be right behind you!"

I hesitated.

"Now!" Jack screamed.

This was still too crazy. If I didn't jump far enough to get clear, the back wheels of the bus would crush me.

"Get off before I toss you off!"

That might have been easier.

"Now! Jump and roll!"

There was no more time to wait. I jumped, trying to get as far away as possible. I was flying through the air like a bird, and then I hit the ground and spun and rolled and rolled, head over feet, finally coming to a stop, my face plowing into the soil. I tried to push myself up but the wind had been knocked out of me. I strained to get air into my lungs, struggled to push myself up onto my knees. I watched the bus continue to roll away ... why hadn't Jack jumped off? Had he jumped and I hadn't seen him, or——? The bus blew up, and I was knocked backwards by the force of the explosion!

CHAPTER FOURTEEN

MY BODY AND FACE were pelted with what felt like pieces of hail! I turned away and covered my face with my hands. There were pieces of metal lying all around everywhere ... they'd showered down around me like shrapnel from a bomb. I'd made it out just in time and—Jack. Where was Jack? Had he jumped off the bus in time?

A figure stood up and staggered toward me out of the dust. It was Jack! His face was cut and his clothes were ripped. His face was black with soot and his eyes were wide open and he had a wild look.

"Are you okay?" I asked.

"What?"

"Are you okay?"

He shook his head. "The bus ... it exploded!" he yelled.

"It was on fire."

"What?"

"It was on fire!" I yelled.

He shook his head. "It ... bus ... it's gone ... it just exploded."

There were sirens, and I turned around to see a plant security vehicle and an ambulance and a fire truck rumbling toward us, red lights flashing. I reached up and grabbed Jack's hand and he pulled me to my feet. He was stunned but he was still strong. We walked away from the wreckage and toward the oncoming emergency vehicles.

The fire truck rolled past while the ambulance and the security vehicle squealed to a stop right in front of us. Immediately the doors sprang open and people jumped out. Mr. Granger was the first, and he ran to our side.

"Boys, are you all right?" he demanded.

"It's Jack ... his ears ... he can't hear."

Mr. Granger called for the ambulance drivers. Jack didn't fight or object as the two men took him, one on each side, and led him away to the waiting ambulance. Mr. Granger took me by the arm and we followed.

"How close was he when the bus exploded?" Mr. Granger asked.

"Close, really close. I was farther away."

"The force of the explosion may have damaged his eardrums. They might have burst."

"He won't be able to hear?" I gasped.

"He'll be fine. It happens sometimes, but they heal quickly."

"Thank God."

They took Jack into the ambulance and had him sit down on the edge of a stretcher. Mr. Granger and I stood at the open back doors.

At that instant a second fire vehicle rumbled up. I turned and watched as it passed and saw the men from the first truck, already out, using their hoses to put out scattered fires.

"What exactly happened?" Mr. Granger asked.

"The bus was on fire," I said. "Under the hood ... the engine. The driver tried to put it out but he couldn't. We knew we had to get it away from the building. Jack jumped behind the wheel and we drove it away."

"Good thing you did," Mr. Granger said.

"I thought it would burn ... that we had to move it because it was a fire risk ... but I didn't think it would explode like that, you know, so big."

"Yes, it was a much bigger explosion than ..." He stopped mid-sentence and turned to the ambulance attendants. "How's he doing?"

"Some cuts to the scalp and maybe a burst eardrum—"

"Nothing more serious?"

"No, he's going to be fine."

"Good. Take him to my office."

"We should be taking him to the infirmary to be—"

"Take him to my office, now!" Mr. Granger ordered. "Then you'll take him to the hospital. Understand?"

"Yes, sir," the attendant said.

Another attendant jumped out the back of the ambulance and slammed the two doors closed. He then ran around the side, jumped into the driver's seat and set the vehicle in motion, sirens blaring and lights flashing.

"George, it wasn't just the bus exploding. It was the dynamite," Mr. Granger said.

"No, we got it away from the dynamite. It was the engine, it was on fire, that's why it exploded."

"Smell," he said, and he inhaled deeply.

I sniffed the air. There was an odour of smoke and fire. Was that what he meant?

"That's the unmistakable smell of dynamite," Mr. Granger said. "And, judging by the extent of the wreckage and the size of the crater that the explosion caused, I would suspect that it was at least twenty or thirty—"

"George!"

I turned around. It was Daphne.

"Jack … is he … is he …?"

"He's in the ambulance, but he's fine," I said.

"Thank goodness!"

She looked genuinely relieved. Maybe she really did care for him.

"Here." She handed me the camera.

"Thanks."

"Have him call me as soon as he can," she said. "I'll be worried until I hear."

"I'll have him call. He'll talk to you," I said. *Although he might not be able to hear you*, I thought.

"Please excuse us, but we have to leave," Mr. Granger said to Daphne. He turned to me. "You're with me."

Mr. Granger walked over to his car. I ran after him and jumped in the passenger side as he climbed in behind the wheel. The lights and siren on the top of his car were still going. He turned the siren off.

"I've seen her around the plant, but I can't place her. Who was that?" he asked.

"Daphne. Remember from the bingo night? She's a friend of my brother's."

"Aah, yes, I remember."

"Yeah, and she was there with us when we saw that the bus was on fire."

"She seemed very interested," he said.

"That's because they're sort of girlfriend and boyfriend."

"Sort of?"

"I guess they are."

"She looks older."

"She is. She's seventeen, and she *thinks* Jack is seventeen."

He nodded. "But why did she have a camera?"

"It's my camera ... well, *The Commando*'s camera. I had it with me in case I saw something that would make a good story."

"You certainly saw something. Did you get any pictures of it?" he asked.

"A couple. At least I think I did."

"I'll take the camera and develop the film. You never know what we might find."

Mr. Granger turned the car around and I looked out the window. Between the emergency vehicles with their flashing lights and the firemen dousing the scattered fires, the whole scene was unbelievable. I tried to see if there were any parts of the bus that I could recognize as parts of a bus. Nothing. If the explosion did that to the bus, what would have happened to us if we hadn't bailed out? A shiver went up my spine.

"I thought that bus was only used for transporting people," I said.

"It is."

"So why was there dynamite on board? Don't they use trucks to transport stuff like that?"

"We do use trucks."

"You shouldn't let them put dangerous materials on the buses."

"George, we didn't *let* anybody. That fire, the dynamite, that was all planned. Those were acts of sabotage."

"Sabotage? Are you sure?"

"I'll know more once we complete our interviews and examine the wreckage. We have a team coming in from Camp X right now."

"You should double the men at the gates," I said.

"Doesn't that seem like shutting the barn door after the cow has escaped?"

"It's not a cow, and it's not escaping I was thinking about," I said. "This would be the perfect distraction to allow somebody to bring in something that they shouldn't."

Mr. Granger was about to speak but he stopped. He grabbed the car radio instead.

"This is Granger to communications," he said into the microphone. "I want all deliveries, I repeat, *all deliveries* held at the gates until further notice." He replaced the microphone. "You almost got yourself killed and you're still thinking about plant security. Are you sure you're only twelve?"

"Pretty sure."

"You came very close to never seeing thirteen," he said.

We pulled up to an open parking spot beside the ambulance. Jack was being led away by the attendants. He brushed away their assistance. That was like Jack. Obviously he was feeling a little bit more like himself. We caught up to them as they started up the stairs toward Mr. Granger's office.

"You two wait downstairs," Mr. Granger said to the attendants. "You'll take him to the hospital as soon as I'm through with the debriefing."

Jack was holding a large piece of gauze to the side of his head. It was soaked with blood, but at least it looked as though the flow had stopped. We walked into the outer office. There was a young girl sitting behind a desk working away on a typewriter. She looked up from her work and I skidded to a stop—it was Juliette!

"You work for Mr. Granger?" I asked.

"You two know each other?" Mr. Granger questioned.

"We're practically engaged," she said. She started to laugh, and then her expression changed to shock as she saw Jack.

"Jack, are you okay?"

Jack had that same stunned look on his face, but he smiled at her. I wondered if he'd even heard the question.

"What happened?" she asked.

"That's what we're going to find out," Mr. Granger said.

"Yes … yes, sir."

"I don't want to be interrupted. Hold my calls." He stopped. "Except from my good friend Bill."

Of course he'd want to talk to Bill. *I* wanted to talk to Bill.

"And does Bill have a last name?" Juliette asked.

"I think everybody has a last name," Mr. Granger replied. "But Bill is the only name he ever needs to give to you. Do you understand?"

"Yes, sir."

He opened the door and ushered us into the office. He pulled up two chairs and set them right in front of his desk, and we sat down.

"You boys seem to know everybody at this plant," Mr. Granger said.

"Not everybody. Juliette is a friend of Daphne's."

"What an interesting coincidence."

The way he said "coincidence" made me think that he was wondering if there was more to it than that. Being the head of security probably made him question everything and everybody. I knew that feeling well.

"How long has Juliette been your secretary?" I asked.

"Not long. She's filling in this week while my regular secretary is away on holidays. She's done a fine job. She's bright ... excellent typist ... can take dictation. You look surprised."

I was a bit surprised that Juliette was such a skilled secretary—I hadn't really seen her that way. But that's not what I told him. "I guess I'm surprised that they'd put somebody kind of new in as your secretary. I thought everything you did would be pretty top secret."

"She deals only with things that are routine. The inside

information—knowledge about the operatives in the plant, for example—is kept securely away from even my regular secretary."

"Of course, I should have known. Sorry, it's just that my brother says I see spies everywhere."

"Welcome to the club. Now, back to what we need to discuss. Tell me what happened."

"There's not much more to tell. We were sitting outside and saw the bus was on fire."

"Where was the fire?"

"Under the hood, in the engine. There was lots of black smoke, and then, when the driver popped the hood, we saw lots of flames. How is he?"

"Second-degree burns on both hands, but he'll be fine."

"And you think the fire was deliberately set, right?"

"No question."

"But how would somebody do that? It's not like the driver wouldn't have noticed somebody going under the hood."

"The trigger might have been placed there the night before, and then as the engine heated up it set off a small charge that ignited the fire."

"What about the dynamite?"

"That could have been anywhere on the bus. It could have been as simple as somebody leaving a bag underneath a seat, or wrapping it underneath the body of the vehicle, and then the heat from the fire finally ignited it."

"But where would somebody get——?" I stopped myself as I realized how silly that question was. We were surrounded by dynamite and explosives. Hundreds of people had daily access to explosives.

"It would be child's play to either bring in individual pieces or abscond with them from our supplies," Mr. Granger said, confirming my thoughts. "I hardly like to think what would have happened if that bus had exploded among the buildings."

"It would have been bad." Maybe that was an under-statement!

"You boys really are heroes."

"Thanks," I mumbled.

"What?" Jack asked loudly. He hadn't bothered trying to follow the conversation.

"Heroes!" I yelled at him. "You're a hero!"

"Oh, yeah, okay ... thanks."

Jack dug his index finger into his right ear and started working away, trying to make his ear work.

"I'm sorry, Jack. We'll get you to a doctor," Mr. Granger said very loudly. Then he turned to me. "I guess, under the circumstances, I'll have to talk to your brother later to find out what he saw. One thing's for sure, though——having you two at the plant was an excel-lent idea. Do you know how many lives you saved today?"

"No idea," I said.

"Neither do I, but it could have been dozens, maybe hundreds. If that explosion had ignited a building, the whole plant could have gone up."

"Wow."

Jack continued to dig his finger into his ear. He was shaking his head, turning it from side to side as if he were trying to get water out of it.

"But now we have another problem," he said.

"We do?"

"Within a few minutes every employee in the whole plant will know what you did. Do you know what that means?"

I shook my head.

"People are going to be looking at you. It's hard for you to observe anybody else when you're being watched by everybody. Your effectiveness has been severely compromised."

"But maybe you don't need us any more," I said.

"I don't follow."

"Maybe that was their plan, and now that we've stopped them they won't know what to do next."

"The failure of this attempt might slow them down temporarily, but now we know that our suspicions were correct. There definitely are enemy agents operating within the facility. That was no outside attempt. That was internal sabotage."

He was right. What had happened had only confirmed what they feared—the reason they had us here.

"And, of course, what you did is going to make those people very unhappy—unhappy with you and your brother."

A ripple of electricity went up my spine. We'd no longer simply be hunters. We might now become the hunted.

CHAPTER FIFTEEN

I STUDIED THE FRONT PAGE of the latest edition of *The Commando*. It was posted on the bulletin board of the building I worked in, and in every other building around the facility.

There, above the fold, was one of the pictures I'd taken of the burning bus. It was a good picture. But that was the only thing in the whole article that was real. The story was about how the bus had overheated, resulting in a fire in the engine. It went on to say that three people, "the driver and two passengers who were on the bus," had suffered "minor injuries" and that the bus itself was "beyond repair." I guess that was true since it was now in a few thousand little pieces, none much bigger than the size of a seat cushion.

It wasn't so much what it *did* say as what it *didn't*. There was no mention of sabotage, dynamite, Jack driving the bus away or our names at all. My first chance at a big story—a story I'd witnessed myself—and I didn't get to write it. Mr. Chalmers wrote it, but he only wrote what he'd been told by Mr. Granger, and that was what Bill had told him to say. I'd learned that Bill was a master at making up stories on the fly. When he told the story it was so real, with so much detail, that if I hadn't been there myself I certainly would have believed him. After the war was over I could see him becoming a famous author, maybe writing spy stories—who knows, they might even become movies. I could picture Little Bill as some sort of secret agent guy, cool, calm and lethal. Then again, I knew nobody would ever write about any of this. The Official Secrets Act would make sure all this secret agent stuff stayed secret.

I knew the truth and I knew this was all a lie, but I figured in this case lying made sense. There was no need to worry the people in the plant, and it was best to down-play what Jack and I had done. There was no point in drawing any more attention to us, and this story kept us out of the picture. Really, not many people had seen us at the scene. There'd been only a few people standing by the bus, and then it had all happened so fast and we'd got far away pretty quickly. When the bus did blow up there'd been nobody out there in that field but Jack and me. And if it had blown up a few seconds earlier, we would still have been out there in the field … scattered around in little pieces so small you wouldn't have known they were parts of a person.

At least that's what Bill had told us when he'd led our debriefing the next day. Most of Jack's hearing had come back by then, but he didn't have much more to add to what I'd already told Mr. Granger. Bill confirmed most of what Mr. Granger had suspected. There had been something rigged under the engine and there had been dynamite on board. What Mr. Granger had wrong was the amount. Bill figured it had to have been almost forty pieces to create a crater that big.

I'd wanted to go back out and have a look at the site, but so far, I hadn't. That way it didn't seem as real, and it was probably better that way.

There was really only one person who knew what we'd done, and that was Daphne. She had seen the two of us get on the bus. Mr. Granger had asked her not to talk about it to anybody and she'd agreed, although she told us she wasn't happy that people wouldn't know that her "Jackie" was a hero. If the two of them had been all goo-goo eyes before this, they were much worse now.

Daphne had been at the infirmary waiting when Jack was finally brought there. She'd stayed until almost the second my mother arrived. I'd thought for sure she was going to stick around to meet her, but no. It was probably better that way. That wouldn't have been the best time for the two of them to meet.

My mother was not happy. Once again she'd walked into a hospital room to see one of her boys all banged up. This time, though, she was told what had really happened. And that made it a lot harder. I wondered if she was feeling guilty because this time she'd been the one that got us into everything. But there was nothing I could do about that.

It looked as though people were buying the story in the paper. Nobody came up and talked to Jack or me about it. People didn't realize that we were the "two passengers." I figured that made us less of a target and better able to keep doing our jobs—watching, not being watched. So far it looked like it was working. And now I had another story to research.

I pushed open the door to the factory floor and peeked in. Stretching out in front of me were five gigantic assembly lines. Women—hundreds and hundreds of women—were standing on either side of long, thin conveyor belts. Shells, each about the size of a thermos, moved down the line, but instead of warm chicken noodle soup being poured inside it was a deadly mixture of explosives. These shells were called twenty-five-pounders and they came in three types—smoke, armour-piercing and high explosive.

The women had their hair pinned up under bandanas made of colourful pieces of material. It was like a rainbow, like a flock of parrots. They really stood out because they added practically the only colour to the room. Everybody had on white or grey overalls and almost everything was painted to match. The people running the plant were interested in things being clean and sanitary, but not necessarily pretty.

The only other splashes of colour in the room were the posters on the walls. They were pictures of men in uniform with headings like "EACH TO OUR PART, EACH TO OUR STATION" or "THEY CAN'T DO THEIR JOB UNLESS WE DO OUR PART." The posters were there to promote worker production and morale. People had to know that what they did here was helping to win the war. Those posters were what had given me the inspiration for this column I was writing about working hard on the line.

As the women worked there was constant conversation and laughter, which was louder than the noise of the machinery. It always struck me as strange. Here they were working on high explosives, deadly shells that would be used to kill people, and it was like they were at a social club.

Stranger yet, I'd be around lines where everybody was singing. Often it would be popular songs, but I'd heard whole lines singing church hymns. Somehow praising God and creating ammunition didn't quite fit. Or maybe it fit really well, since some of those shells were going to send our enemies to meet their maker.

Although a lot of the women were married, nobody wore a wedding ring. All jewellery, all metal, had to be left in their lockers. They couldn't risk anything, even the static from a belt buckle, causing a spark. The women had to wear rubber-soled shoes for the same reason.

Mr. Chalmers had asked me to come and write a story about what it was like to work on the line. I'd write it, but what I was really there to do was find enemy agents. Thinking about it, though, what were the chances of me wandering through this plant and finding out anything anyway? It wasn't like the enemy agent would be goose-stepping around or yelling out "*Heil Hitler!*" as I passed by.

I walked down the line, looking at the ladies working on the shells. Occasionally I'd get a smile or a nod, but most were too busy talking to the women across from them, and of course working, to notice me.

I got to the end and turned around, walking back between two different lines, which actually looked identical. I couldn't imagine doing what these women were doing all day long. No wonder they spent so much time laughing and talking. They had to do something to break the monotony. Nothing more to see here, I figured.

Back in the lobby, the picture of the bus in the paper again caught my eye. That bus had cost me more sleep … like I could afford to lose more sleep. I took my jacket from the coat rack by the door—I'd had to leave it there because it had metal buttons—and left.

It was cold outside, colder than I would have expected for the middle of November. It was below freezing, but the way the wind was whipping along it felt much colder. The sun was up there somewhere in the sky, but the clouds were blocking it from view, so it didn't provide any relief. It almost looked like it was going to start to … thick flakes of snow began to swirl out of the sky.

I turned the collar of my coat up. I wished I had brought mitts and a hat or boots, or at least shoes that didn't have a hole in the toe. Up ahead was a building I'd never been inside. If I walked in the front door and out the back I could at least be out of the weather for a while. I didn't know what they did in there, but I did know it would be warmer, and it definitely wouldn't be snowing inside.

I opened the door and was hit by a wave of fumes. This had to be one of the mixing buildings, a place where they combined different chemicals to create the explosives.

"Hello, son, can I help you?" asked the guard. He had a rifle on his back and was standing by the door that led to the shop floor.

"I'm with *The Commando*," I said. "I'm a reporter."

"You?"

I pulled out the letter that was signed by Mr. Chalmers and Mr. Granger. It gave me permission to go anywhere I wanted. I handed it to the guard.

"I don't seem to be able to find my glasses," he said as he fumbled around, patting his pockets.

I pointed up to the top of his head where they were perched.

"Lose my head if it wasn't attached."

That was the sort of thing that always made me nervous. Guards who couldn't find their glasses might not be able to see other things that were right under their eyes.

"I guess they're really scraping the bottom of the barrel when they have old men as guards and kids as reporters," he said.

"I guess so."

He handed me back the letter. "You can go in there," he said, gesturing to the door, "but are you sure you want to?"

I gave him a questioning look.

"Son, if you think the smell out here is bad, wait till you go inside there. Be my guest."

Tentatively I pushed the door open and the smell practically knocked me off my feet. I cringed and stepped back, letting the door close.

"I'm hoping I'll be going to Heaven, but either way I have a pretty good idea what it smells like in Hell," the guard said.

"What are they doing in there?" I asked as I peered in through the small window in the door.

"See those large vats?" he asked.

I nodded.

"They contain different chemicals. Nitrates, fulminate of mercury, toluene and nitroglycerine."

"Nitroglycerine I've heard of," I said. "It's really dangerous, isn't it?"

"Everything in there is really dangerous. A regular witch's brew of everything ever made that can cause an explosion. That's why they have a guard stationed here. You sure you want to go in?"

I shrugged. "Maybe not ... maybe another day."

"Wise choice, son. I pity those men who have to spend their days in there working. Even with those masks they wear, it still can't be a good thing for them to—"

He stopped as the outside door opened and another guard came in.

"You're late!" he called out to him.

"Two minutes." He stomped his feet and brushed snow off the shoulders of his coat. "Snowing like crazy out there," he said.

We both walked over to the door as though, despite the

snow he'd brought in, we didn't believe him. The snow was coming down so thick that I could hardly see the buildings in the distance, and the ground was already frosted over.

"I think I'd better get myself home while I can," the first guard said.

"I'd better get going too," I said.

I headed out the door with the guard. "I'm not dressed for this," I said, looking down at my shoes.

"We'll try to stay where the snow hasn't settled."

"What does that mean?" I asked.

"Follow me."

He shifted over to the side and I quickly saw what he was talking about. There was a long line, like a dirt path, where no snow had accumulated. Why was it like that?

"I don't understand. Why isn't there snow here?"

"It *will* settle once it snows more."

"But why not now?" I asked.

"Underground pipes carrying steam. The entire facility is heated by steam," he said. "There are pipes that lead from the steam plant to every building. Look, you can see where they are."

He was right, I *could* see them. Each building was joined to the next by a thin strip, a path of clear ground that could now be seen as it stood out against the snow. The whole plant was designed so that the buildings were all separate—that was for safety reasons—but really, they weren't separate. They were all connected.

"And this steam plant ... where is it?" I asked.

"It's back there," he said, waving a hand in the direction we'd come from.

"Where? Where, exactly, is it?"

"On the edge of the property," he said without looking back.

I grabbed him by the arm. "Where?"

He looked surprised and annoyed. I let go of his arm.

"See those smokestacks?" he said.

I looked through the snow. I could see two stacks in the distance.

"Okay ... thanks." I started walking toward them.

"Kid!" he called after me. "Kid!"

I turned around and waved to him. I couldn't tell him why, but I needed to see the steam plant up close.

CHAPTER SIXTEEN

THE SNOW WAS FALLING fast and thick, but not so fast or so thick that it could cover up the telltale signs that there were heated pipes running underneath the ground. They'd been there all the time, of course, but I'd never been able to notice them before. Now they were so obvious. Here at the munitions plant—where they made a point of spreading things out, of making sure that there were many separate and separated buildings—there was this one connection to *all* of the buildings!

As I got closer to the steam plant I started to wonder how I'd never really noticed it before. It was big, grey, solid and topped by two large chimneys, from which thick smoke rose up and disappeared into the snowy sky. I circled around the building, looking for a way in. At the side there were two large trucks parked. The big garage doors were closed but there was a little door beside them. I turned the knob and the door opened and I walked in.

The garage was cavernous—big, with the ceiling high above—and with the exception of another two trucks it was empty. It felt good to get out of the snow, but it really wasn't that much warmer in here. I could still see my breath, which was coming in puffs. I needed to slow down, both my breath and my pounding heart.

I walked between the trucks and looked around. I couldn't see anybody.

"Hello?" I tentatively called out. There was no answer except for my voice echoing back to me.

I walked to the end where I saw a door. That had to lead somewhere. I pushed it open and was instantly hit by a wave of heat and a rush of sound—loud machinery rhythmically pounding and pumping. I stepped inside and closed the door behind me. It was incredibly hot. It was as if I'd stepped from one season to another, going from bitter winter to tropical summer on opposite sides of the door. The only similarity was that there was nobody here, either. This was perfect—perfect if I wanted to break in and destroy the building.

There was a long corridor that seemed to run around the perimeter of the building, with doors leading off it. I started to check them as I passed. Each one was locked. At least that was some form of security. I kept checking

them, though, like I was some sort of unofficial watch-
man. Passing by the tenth or eleventh door I turned the
knob and found an unlocked door! I hesitated for a few
seconds and then pulled it open.

I walked in and found myself face to face with four
men, sitting around a table playing cards. They all looked
up at me, and they seemed as surprised to see me as I felt
to find them. I had to fight the urge to wave, close the
door and run away.

One of them got up from the table and walked toward
me. He didn't look happy. And I realized how little he
was—he was shorter than me.

"You should not be here!" he stated loudly. He had a
foreign accent of some kind. "Why are you here?"

"I'm allowed to be anywhere." I pulled out the permission letter from my pocket. "I'm a reporter with *The
Commando*."

He practically ripped the letter from my hands and
started to read it. Another of the men got up and came
over—he was much bigger than either the first man or
me. He began reading the letter over the first man's
shoulder.

"You're a reporter?" the second man asked. "You don't
look old enough to know all of your alphabet yet."

The two men still seated laughed, while the first
continued to study the letter. Finally he looked up. "It is

true ... it says he is a reporter and he can go to all areas of the plant."

"Wait a second," the second man said. "I think I read an article you wrote. Isn't your father a pilot?"

"Yes, he is," I said, keeping my cover story alive. I was getting pretty good at lying without a hint of hesitation.

"And you wrote about how all of us back here are just as important because without us the soldiers and sailors and fliers can't do their jobs."

"I wrote that."

"That was a good article. You're a good writer, kid."

"Thanks. And I was thinking that I could write a story about the steam plant."

"There is nothing for you to write about here," the little man said. "You should go."

"Hold your horses there, Case, and let the lad explain himself."

"I thought that I would write about how the steam plant is the heart of the whole facility."

"The heart?" the bigger man asked.

"Yes, the same way the heart pumps blood to keep the body alive, the steam plant pumps out heat to keep the facility alive," I explained.

"Well, I like that," the bigger man said. He turned to the other two, who were sitting. "How do you like that, boys? We're the heart!"

They both smiled and nodded.

"It's about time we got a little recognition. It seems the only time people notice we exist is when something goes wrong," the bigger man said. "What would you like to know?"

"Everything about the——"

"We don't have time for any of this!" the first man, Case, snapped. "We have too much work to do!"

The other three looked at him with a combination of surprise and amusement.

"Come on, Case, I think we can take a few minutes away from our card game to tell him some things about——"

"I think he should leave, *immediately*, and we should get back to our work!"

"And I think that you're not my boss and you should stop trying to be one!" the big man said. He took a step forward until he was standing almost over top of the smaller man.

"Then maybe I should find the foreman and inform him that you three are playing cards."

"You do that, and you be sure to tell him who was sitting in that fourth chair playing along with us. Now, either quiet down or push off!"

Case snorted and then turned and stomped off, pushing past me to get through the door.

"I'm ... I'm sorry," I stammered. "I didn't mean to cause any trouble."

"You didn't, kid. Case got a burr under his saddle for some reason. Those Norwegians can be like that ... stubborn people. Now, what do you want to know?"

"But what about the foreman?"

"I can tell you more than he can."

"No, I mean, aren't you worried about him coming here and finding you playing cards?"

"No worries. It's not like they're going to be firing any of us. We're three of the engineers who keep this place going. Come on, I'll give you a tour and answer your questions at the same time. My name is Frank," he said, and he offered me his hand.

"I'm George."

"I know that," he said. "It says so in the letter."

I followed him out of the little room and back into the corridor. Almost immediately he began explaining how the plant worked. He was using a lot of technical terms and big words, and while I didn't really understand I nodded my head enthusiastically.

We walked along the corridor and through a door that led us into an enormous room, in the middle of which was a gigantic tank sort of thing that looked like my mother's pressure cooker—except it was as big as a barn.

"This here is the central boiler," he said. "If the steam plant is the heart of the whole facility, then you're looking at the *actual* heart."

He went on explaining in detail how it worked. Again, too many big and technical words for me to understand, but I was getting the information I wanted to find out.

"I was wondering, if this boiler were damaged, what would happen?"

"Simple. The pressure would drop and the whole facility would lose steam and thereby lose heat."

"And would that be dangerous?"

"Dangerous?"

"Would anything explode or anything?"

He laughed. "It would only get cold, here and everywhere else."

"I guess that isn't so dangerous."

"Not that there isn't some danger from other things," he said.

"What sort of other things?"

"Well, you put anything under enough pressure and an explosion is possible." He thumped the boiler and there was a deep, echoing sound. "Tens of thousands of gallons of water, superheated to create steam. If this shell were ruptured, then scalding water and steam would shoot out, along with chunks of metal from the shattered boiler itself. It would kill anybody in this building who was standing too close."

Involuntarily I stepped back, and he laughed.

"You'd have to get a lot farther away than that! But no worries, it's as safe as houses in here. First sign of any trouble and the pressure would be released through valves—no chance of anything bad happening."

I felt relieved. I looked up to the top of the boiler. Leading out of it were gigantic pipes. It looked like a big mechanical octopus.

"And those are the pipes that lead to the other buildings, right?"

"Every building on the whole complex."

"What would happen if the pipes in one of the other buildings were damaged or broken?"

"That building would lose heat."

"But it wouldn't explode or anything, would it?"

"No explosion. They'd call us and we'd be over there lickety-split to repair it."

"And what if it didn't break in one of the buildings but underground, leading to the building?"

"That would be more difficult," he said.

"Because you'd have to dig all around to try to find the spot?"

"Because I'd have to go and find Case and apologize," he said.

"I don't understand."

"Come on and I'll show you."

I wasn't crazy about going to find Case, but I followed. We left the boiler behind and walked through a series of doors until we were standing in the corridor by the outside wall. Through the windows at the top I could see that the snow was now falling more heavily.

Frank bent down and lifted up a metal trap door.

"This is one of the places where pipes lead out of the building."

I bent down to look. I could see four thick pipes, white and wrapped in what almost looked like bandages, leading away and into the distance, finally disappearing into the darkness.

"Do you see the service corridor?"

I peered down into the hole. There, beneath the pipes, was an opening, not much more than a little crawl space. I couldn't help but think back to Camp 30, to the tunnel that led out of the camp and across the road ... the tunnel that the prisoners had dug to escape ... the tunnel that Jack and I had been forced to crawl through ... the tunnel that still haunted my sleep. I leaned back and away.

"The pipes are held in service corridors. If there are any problems we would have to go down through these to find it."

"You couldn't fit through that," I said, shaking my head.

"It's unbelievably tight for me, and I don't like closed-in places, but I have gone through these ... not this one, but some of them. That's why I'd be apologizing to Case. He can fit down there. He's a moody sort of fella, but lately he's been doing all the work in the service corridors."

"Have there been a lot of leaks?"

"Not leaks. Maintenance and inspections. Each pipe needs to be inspected each month, and Case has volunteered to do *all* the inspections."

"These corridors lead to every building, right?"

"Every building. He's been crawling through *miles* of corridor. Nasty work. Dark, with only a flashlight, tight spaces, damp, even wet, dirty and full of unexpected surprises."

"What sort of surprises?"

"Mainly rats."

I shuddered. I didn't like rats.

"They don't seem to bother Case."

Actually, he kind of looked like a rat—a rat that had access to every building in the facility.

"I should be going," I said. "Thanks for the tour."

"Do you have enough information for your story?"

"I have everything I need."

"So when should I expect it?" he asked.

"Expect what?"

"The story. When will it be in the paper?"

"Oh, yeah, probably next week … or the week after that. Thanks for your time, and I'm sorry I disturbed your card game."

"No worry. There'll be lots of time for us to play Skat."

"You were playing Skat?" I exclaimed before I could stop myself.

"You've heard of it?" He sounded equally surprised.

"Yes ... from my grandparents," I lied.

"Are your grandparents Norwegian?"

"No," I said, shaking my head. Why would he think that?

"Case taught it to us. He said it was very popular in Norway."

It was also popular in Germany. That was the card game the German prisoners played at Camp 30. Maybe it was played in Norway, too. Maybe Case *was* Norwegian. Maybe none of this meant anything. Maybe. Maybe not.

CHAPTER SEVENTEEN

THE WIND practically blew me back into the building. During my time inside, the snowstorm had grown into a full-blown blizzard. Now all the ground was covered, including the strips above the heating pipes. The evidence had disappeared; the pipes were once again invisible to the naked eye. But though it couldn't be seen, the danger still remained.

The storm outside was no more blustery than the storm inside my head. I was struggling to figure out how much of what I was thinking was simply me overreacting. Maybe Skat was a popular card game in lots of countries. What did I know about what they did in Norway? And, of course, Bill must know about the pipes and the service corridors. And if he didn't know, then I was sure Mr. Granger would … that's who I needed to talk to. I changed directions and headed toward his office.

Now I was walking straight into the wind, and I could feel it right through my clothes, biting down to the bone. I turned up the collar of my coat and pulled my hands inside my sleeves. Head down, I trudged forward. Why did the steam plant have to be so far from his office— from everything? By the time I got there my teeth would be chattering so much I wouldn't be able to tell him anything. I passed building after building, some offering a little shelter from the wind, until I saw Mr. Granger's up ahead. There was a truck parked there and his car, the one he'd driven me in after the bus explosion. That was good—he was in. It would have been awful to walk all this way for nothing.

I stepped inside. Instant relief from the cold and snow. I stomped the snow off my shoes. The big toe on one foot—the one that had the shoe with the hole in it—felt prickly and numb. Not a great sign.

I walked up the stairs and then hesitated at the door that led to his office. What exactly was I going to say to him? Was this worth anything, or was this an example of me being shell shocked—seeing a spy behind every bush and card game? Maybe it was nothing more than coincidence ... what was it that Bill always said ... that he didn't like coincidences? Neither did I.

I opened the door and walked in. I was startled to see Juliette sitting at the reception desk. Somehow it had slipped my mind that she was there. Not a pleasant surprise.

"So, Georgie, you couldn't keep yourself away and you've come to see me!" She beamed.

"I've come to see somebody but it isn't you."

"Now you're hurting my feelings."

"Is Mr. Granger in?"

Before she could answer, the phone rang and she gestured for me to wait.

"Mr. Granger's office," she sang out.

As she listened I noticed that her usual expression—that sort of smug, silly grin—faded away. She turned in her seat so that she faced away from me, mumbled something in reply and then returned the phone to its cradle.

"You wanted to see Mr. Granger?" she asked, suddenly sounding very serious.

"Yes."

"He's not in," she said.

"But his car is outside," I said.

"I guess he didn't take that car. He only uses it around the facility, and he's left for the day."

"Already? It's only five-thirty."

"Sometimes he leaves even earlier," she said.

"He does?" He'd told me that he was practically sleeping here these days.

"He's the boss. He can leave whenever he wants."

"But why are you still here?" I asked.

"I'm *not* the boss. I have to finish my work, and I'd better get back to it. Is there anything else?"

"I guess not."

"The sooner I do my work, the sooner I can leave. So, if you'll excuse me ..." She suddenly spun her chair away from me toward a typewriter table and started typing. I stood there, staring at her, feeling as though I'd been dismissed. I *had* been dismissed.

I walked out the door. Something didn't seem right. First, Mr. Granger had told me that he was at the office pretty much around the clock these days, and his car was here, but he was gone? Maybe he'd be coming back later on. I turned around and went back through the door. Juliette was on the phone now, and her eyes widened in surprise. She looked like a little kid who'd been caught with her hand in the cookie jar.

She hung up the phone without saying goodbye.

"Yes?" she asked.

"Could I please leave a message for Mr. Granger?"

"Certainly."

Suddenly I realized that I didn't really know what message I wanted to give—and more important, I didn't want to give any message to her.

"Yes?" she asked.

"Could you tell him that I was here and that I wanted to see him ... okay?"

"I'll pass on that message, but remember, he's a very busy man and he might not have time to get back to you for at least a few days."

"Sure ... thanks."

I left the office again. This was all strange. Who had she been talking to, and why had she hung up when she saw me? Was I now picturing Juliette as an enemy agent? She was probably on the phone with some boy ... maybe she had called Daphne ... was she a spy, too? I really had to rein in my imagination.

I went down the stairs and back outside. The storm seemed to be stronger now—or maybe it felt that way because I'd been inside. No, it really *was* stronger. I could barely see the buildings on either side of me through the snow.

I plowed forward, head down, trudging toward the gate and toward home. I had to get home. I had to tell my mother and brother what I'd seen. I needed to have their opinion and their help. If I couldn't tell Mr. Granger any of this, I had to tell Bill. Maybe it was a bunch of nothing, but he was the one who could decide.

Suddenly I heard the roar of an engine behind me. I turned around and there was a truck—a gigantic truck— bearing right down on me! I leaped to the side, landing face first in the snow as it raced past me!

It didn't stop or slow down. In all this snow, the driver hadn't seen me. The taillights of the truck disappeared into the blizzard. I picked myself up and brushed off the snow. I had to get home, and I had to be careful. If he hadn't seen me, then nobody else on the road would, either.

Then I had a terrible thought. Maybe he *had* seen me—maybe he was *trying* to hit me. Either way, I had to be careful.

CHAPTER EIGHTEEN

"I'M NOT GOING to be surprised if you come down with pneumonia," my mother said, as she rubbed my head vigorously with a towel. I had the feeling she was rubbing a lot harder than she had to just to get my hair dry because she was so angry with me.

"I feel good," I said. And I did feel good. I was warm and I'd changed into dry clothes.

"I don't know what you were thinking," she continued.

"I was thinking that I had to get home, and I wasn't going to wait for spring."

"Don't give me any backtalk," she warned.

"Sorry. But I had to do something important."

"Nothing is as important as the health of my boys. It's bad enough that Jack isn't well."

"I'm perfectly fine now," Jack said. "I can probably go back to work tomorrow."

Jack had already missed three days, but now his hearing was almost good as new.

"*Maybe* you can go back to work," my mother warned.

"But the doctor said I'd be fine."

"I don't care about the doctor. It's what your mother thinks that's important. Now, let me put the kettle on and fix you both a cup of tea."

"Thanks. That would be nice."

She went to the kitchen, and Jack leaned in close to me.

"So, what's so important?" he asked.

"Wait!" my mother yelled from the kitchen. "I want to hear everything too."

She returned, and in a burst I told them about the steam plant, the pipes and the service corridors that led to all the buildings, about Case, and I ended by telling them about the Skat game. I was also very deliberate in what I *didn't* mention—almost being hit by the truck. That was important, but not important enough to get my mother worried.

"That's very interesting," my mother said. "But it might mean nothing."

"It might … or it might not," I said. "I think I have to tell Bill."

"I'm sure he'll be interested. But I'm not sure when we'll see him again—"

"No, we have to tell him now, right away," I insisted.

"Tonight?"

"Yes, tonight. We have to go to Camp X."

"Unless you've forgotten, there's a storm outside, and it's gotten worse since you got home. We're not going anywhere."

"But we *have* to go!"

"George, even if we had a car we couldn't drive in this weather. It will have to wait until tomorrow at the earliest."

"But what if tomorrow is too late?" I protested. "Remember what Bill said? Reports have been telling him that an attack could happen any time now."

"And then the bus exploded," she said.

This wasn't getting me anywhere. I turned to Jack. "What do you think?"

"I think this might mean nothing," he said. "It might be nothing more than a big, fat coincidence."

This wasn't the support I was hoping for.

"But," he continued, "it might mean *everything*. George is right, Mom. We can't keep this to ourselves. We have to tell Bill and let him decide what's important."

"Yes, but even if George *is* right," my mother said, "there's no way we can tell Bill right away. The phone is out of the question, for security reasons. We can't drive to the camp. And it's not as though we can walk there."

She had a point. It looked as though our hands were tied.

"What if you talked to Mr. McGregor?" she suggested.

"Mr. McGregor?"

"He seems to be in communication with Bill, and he does have a car."

"You're right," I agreed. "Could Jack and I go over to his house and——?"

I was stopped mid-sentence by a loud knocking on the front door.

"Who could that be?" my mother asked. "It's not fit out there for man nor beast."

For a split second I had the strangest thought that it was Bill at the door. He had a knack for showing up right when we needed him most.

"Whoever it is, they'll certainly want out of the storm."

My mother went to the door and opened it. A small figure, hidden beneath a thick coat and a hood, was blown in through the door along with a shower of snow. My mother fought the wind and closed the door again.

For a fleeting second I had a terrible thought—it was Case underneath that coat and he'd followed me home and ... the hood was pulled down and I was even more shocked.

"Daphne!" Jack exclaimed as he jumped to his feet.

"Hello, Jack, George. And you must be Mrs. Brown," she said as she offered her hand to my mother.

"I'm so pleased to meet you," my mother replied as they shook hands.

"I've been *dying* to meet you!" Daphne said. "Jack talks about you all the time."

"Yes, he mentions you, too," my mother said.

"I have to apologize for coming without an invitation. You must think I'm a terrible person."

"Not at all. I had extended an invitation ... perhaps Jack didn't pass it on?"

Jack looked down at his feet. He didn't look any too comfortable.

"I was just so worried about my Jack."

"Well, you *must* have been worried to come out on such a terrible night. Please, come in, and take your coat off." Right then the kettle began whistling loudly from the kitchen. "I was about to make a pot of tea. You must stay and chat. I have so many questions I'd like to ask you."

Jack went from looking uncomfortable to looking as if he might be sick.

"George," my mother said, "would you please go in and make the tea?"

"But I have to—"

"George?" She shot me a familiar look that let me know this was more like an order than a request. I knew there was no point in arguing. It would be faster to do it than fight about it.

"And Jack, don't just stand there, take Daphne's coat, dear."

I hurried into the kitchen. I didn't mind making the tea, but I didn't want to miss any part of the conversation that was about to take place. I wondered if there was any way Jack could dance fast enough to keep those two from asking questions he didn't want answered.

I took the kettle off the burner and the squealing died down and stopped. I put the tea leaves in the strainer and poured the water through and into the teapot. It would have to steep, but I wasn't going to stand in there and wait. I wanted to be either in the living room listening or out the door going to Mr. McGregor's house.

When I got back to the living room, Jack and Daphne were seated on the chesterfield, side by side. There was a bit of space between them, though—they weren't inter-twined, the way they usually were. That was smart, with my mother watching. She sat on a chair opposite them.

"Jack never did tell me exactly how the two of you met," she began.

"It was at the movies," Daphne said.

"I told you that," Jack said.

"We started talking, and I was so impressed with how mature he is."

"He is very mature," my mother agreed, "for somebody his age."

"Age is only a number," Daphne said. "And what's a year?"

A year? What did she mean by that? As far as she was concerned, Jack was seventeen, so there was no difference in their ages ... unless she had just turned eighteen ... that must have been what she meant.

"So, you're seventeen?" my mother said—she was sticking to Jack's cover story, that he was sixteen.

"That's right," Daphne said.

That could mean only one thing—Jack had told her his real age ... or I guess his real cover-story age ... or something. This was so confusing. I wondered what else he had told her. I shot Jack a look, but he had his head down and he was fidgeting nervously with the crease in his pants.

"You look older than seventeen," my mother said.

"Well, I've always looked grown-up for my age."

"Excuse me," I said. "I'll bring the tea in, but then I think I'll go out and see ... my friend."

"That would be fine, dear," my mother agreed. "It will give us girls a chance to get to know each other better."

Could anyone else hear the edge in her voice? I almost felt sorry for Daphne—she was like a mouse that had been caught by a cagey old cat!

"Oh, no, George!" Daphne said. "Surely you don't want to go out there in the storm! It's terribly cold and windy!"

"He won't be going very far," my mother answered.

"But I hardly *ever* get to see George," Daphne said. "I really think he should stay."

Unexpectedly, Daphne got to her feet and moved to the door so that she was practically blocking me from leaving.

"It seems so rude for him to leave when I've just arrived," she said.

"He's not trying to be rude, and he really must go," my mother said forcefully. "He'll be back shortly."

"And I must insist that he not leave at all," Daphne said.

And that's when she pulled a pistol out of her purse and aimed it right at us.

CHAPTER NINETEEN

WE ALL STARED, stunned, mouths wide open, not moving, not breathing, not believing what we were seeing with our own eyes. This could not be real. That couldn't be a real gun.

"All of you, please sit down," Daphne said politely.

I stood frozen in place.

"Daphne, I don't know what sort of joke you're playing, but this isn't funny," Jack said. He got to his feet.

"It wasn't meant to be funny. This is no joke. Sit down. I really don't want to shoot you. I don't want to shoot any of you, but I will if I have to."

"I'm not doing anything until you explain what's gotten into you," Jack said. He had the serious look I knew so well. He wasn't about to back down.

"Please, Jack, sit down. I really want to explain, and I don't want to hurt anybody. Especially not you."

Her voice and expression had softened so that she sounded and looked friendly. I noticed the gun was still aimed at his chest, though. She held it out in front of her and it was shaking ... her hand was shaking. She was the one holding the gun but she was afraid, too.

"Boys, please sit," my mother said.

I sat down on the chesterfield. Jack still hadn't moved. I reached up and took him by the hand and pulled him down beside me.

"You must all be feeling a bit confused," she said.

"You got that right!" Jack snapped.

"I am not who I have pretended to be," she said. "But then, neither are any of you. I know about your family. I know about how you foiled an attack on Camp X and thwarted an escape from Camp 30."

For a second I thought that Jack must have told her, but judging from the look on his face he was equally shocked.

"I know everything. You boys are not the only people in the intelligence business."

"You mean ... you're ... you're ...?"

"A German agent."

I heard the words and I knew what they meant, but how could it be true?

"Judging from the looks on your faces, you did not suspect a thing," she said. "And as part of my work I had to pretend to be your girlfriend."

Jack now looked hurt.

"I had to pretend that I cared for you," she said, "although, to be honest, I have grown fond of you. You are a fine boy."

"Boy?" Jack asked.

"Yes, a fine fifteen-year-old boy. I felt bad about deceiving you. Who knows, if the circumstances had been different and if I'd been much younger, we might have become girlfriend and boyfriend for real."

"Oh yeah? Do you think I'd be friends with a stinking Nazi traitor?" Jack snarled.

"I am no traitor. I am loyal to my country. Germany."

"You can't be German," Jack said. "You don't have an accent."

"I am German, although I moved to Canada when I was only two. My father was employed by the German embassy in Ottawa and I was raised in this country. He was recalled to Germany when the embassy was closed, when war was declared between our two countries."

"How old are you really?" Jack asked.

"I turned twenty-two shortly before we met. I pretended to be seventeen, the same way you pretended to be sixteen."

"Is Daphne your real name?"

She shook her head. "Liesl is my name. I am sorry that I was forced to deceive you in such a manner. In fact,

when they told me that I was to get to know you better I
thought it was a waste of my time. After all, what could a
fifteen-year-old boy and his younger brother know about
our operation?" She paused. "And then there was today,"
she said, looking at me. "You shouldn't have gone to the
steam plant."

"That's why you're here tonight, isn't it?" I said.

"That, and the trip you made to try to see Mr.
Granger."

I nodded my head. "And you knew about that because
Juliette is another agent."

She didn't answer, but I could tell by her expression
that I was right.

"There's no point trying to deny it," I said. "I know
everything."

"Do you? Do you know we have agents throughout the
facility? On the lines, at the steam plant, even at the gatehouse? Perhaps you don't know as much as you think."

"I do know that whatever is going to happen is going to
happen tonight," I said.

She didn't answer, but her smug look faded.

"And I know it's going to happen around midnight, at
the change of shift."

Now she looked shocked. "How could you know that?"

"I know lots of things." I didn't really *know* it, but I
figured that anyone planning an attack would want to do

it at a shift change when people were coming and going, to take advantage of the confusion.

"We were fortunate that Juliette was able to convince you that Mr. Granger wasn't in his office."

"What?"

"He was right behind that door, and because she was able to persuade you to leave, you weren't able to tell him of your suspicions. You weren't able to tell anybody. And I'm here to make sure you stay silent."

"Are you … are you going to kill us?" I gasped.

"I'm not a killer," she said. "I was ordered to simply detain you until after midnight, after the explosion."

"And what then?" Jack asked. "You're going to say goodnight and sashay out of here?"

"I will be receiving orders as to what is to happen next," she said. "Perhaps you will be tied up and left. In the confusion and turmoil that this will produce, we should be able to simply slip away. We'll be out of the country before anybody thinks to look for you, or us."

"If the whole plant goes up, they're going to be looking for all of us … or at least *parts* of all of us," I said.

She looked as though she didn't understand what I meant.

"We're only one street away from the plant. If it goes up, then this whole house is going to be blown away with it," I told her.

"No, we'll be safe here."

"You go ahead and believe that if you want. But maybe it's not only us your boss wants out of the way. Maybe he's trying to tie up some other loose ends, as well ... like you."

She laughed, but it wasn't very convincing. "I won't listen to anything that you have to say."

"Suit yourself. Are you cold?" I asked.

"No."

"Oh, it's just that your hands are shaking ... I thought that was because of the cold."

She looked down at her hand on the gun and realized I was right. "Maybe I'm still a little cold."

"Do you want a cup of the tea that I made?" I asked.

She looked confused about why I was making the offer.

"We could all use a cup of tea to settle our nerves," I said. "Don't worry, you'll still have the gun. It's not like I'm going to hit you over the head with a sugar cube."

She didn't answer.

"Look, it's only about seven o'clock. We can't just sit here staring at each other for the next five hours, right? A cup of tea would be nice ... it would calm everybody's nerves."

She seemed to be thinking. I had to keep talking, try to sway her decision.

"If you stand right there," I said, pointing to the doorway between the kitchen and the living room, "you can keep an eye on all of us ... okay?"

She nodded her head and I got up. I wasn't sure what good this was going to do but at least I was up and moving. Maybe if she drank enough tea she'd have to go to the washroom and ... great, my escape plan hinged on her having to pee.

I walked slowly to the kitchen, taking care not to make any sudden moves. She trailed behind me, and I was unnerved to see the gun aimed at me, her hand still shaking. I liked her being scared and unsure. I didn't like her being that way with the pistol pointed at me.

"Bring it back in here," she said. "The tea, the cups, everything."

"Sure."

I pulled out a tray and placed it on the counter. I put the teapot onto the tray. Next, beside it, I put the little dish holding the sugar cubes. I pulled some spoons out of the drawer, placing them on the tray as well. Then I opened the fridge and took out the milk. I poured some of it into a little creamer, put that on the tray and returned the rest to the refrigerator. All I needed now were the cups.

"Mom!" I called out. "Do you want me to use the good china cups? After all, we do have company."

I looked at Liesl. Her expression was one of complete and utter bewilderment. I smiled at her. I remembered something that Little Bill had told me once—always be friendly, always smile, when you plan to kill somebody. Not that I was going to be killing her—I still only had sugar cubes and a spoon—but I wanted to act like nothing was wrong, like everything was fine and friendly. I needed to lull her into a false sense of safety.

"Well?" I called out again.

"Use whatever cups you like," my mother answered.

"Thanks."

I went to the cupboard where the good china cups were kept—and there, right beside them, was my mother's envelope full of sleeping powder! I had a rush of inspiration. If I could put that into her tea, it would knock her out ... but how could I get it into her drink and nobody else's? How could I even get it into *her* tea? It wasn't like I could convince her it was sugar or—

"What are you doing in that cupboard?" Daphne demanded.

"Nothing ... I'm trying to decide which cups to use."

"Just take any old cups," she said.

"Sure." I took out two cups and saucers, turned around and placed them on the tray. Liesl was looking right at me. There was no way I could do anything with her watching me that closely. I had to get her to focus somewhere else.

"Liesl, did you ever really like my brother at all?"

"Yeah," Jack called out from the other room.

She turned to face the living room—*away* from me.

"I did—I *do* like you, Jack," she said.

I turned back to the cupboard. I chose another cup and placed the envelope of powder inside it, and then grabbed one more and put them both on the tray. This time I had my back to her, blocking her view.

"I didn't mean to hurt you in any way, Jack," she went on. "I thought that you'd never discover the truth."

What now? I couldn't put the powder into only one of the cups. Everyone would see the powder dissolving—and even if it wasn't noticeable, how could I be sure she'd take the right cup? Instead, I took the top from the teapot and tipped the envelope into it. How much should I pour? Better too much than too little—I dumped it all in. Then I took the empty envelope, folded it over and slipped it into my pocket.

It would be simple enough for me to pretend to drink, but I didn't know how I could warn my brother and mother—I *couldn't*, not without running the risk of tipping off Liesl. I'd have to knock them all out. Better to put everybody out than have Liesl find out what I was doing.

I picked up the tray and turned around. Liesl was still talking to Jack and paying very little attention to me.

"Excuse me," I said.

She started slightly, turned the pistol toward me and then moved out of the doorway and into the living room. She took a seat on the chair farthest away from the chester-field. I walked in and placed the tray on the coffee table.

"I'll pour," I said.

I had to make a quick decision—was it best to serve Daphne first, so she could drink first, or was it better to wait for the powder to dissolve more? I'd put her in the middle.

"Mom, you want sugar and milk, right?"

"Yes, please."

I poured the milk in first. I was counting on it to hide any cloudiness that the powder might produce. Then I poured the tea into the cup. It was steamy and I couldn't see any trace of the powder. Either it had completely dissolved or it was still sitting in the bottom of the teapot. I used the tongs to take one cube and put it in the cup, stirred it, and then handed my mother the cup and saucer.

"Thank you."

"Liesl, how would you like your—?"

"Lots of milk and three sugars," Jack said. "Unless you *lied* about that, too!"

She actually looked hurt by his words.

"Then lots of milk and three sugar cubes is what she'll get," I said.

I was grateful for all the milk and sugar—better to disguise the sight and taste of the powder. Again, I put the milk in first.

"Is that enough?"

She nodded.

I poured in the tea and then added the sugar. I stirred it thoroughly, the spoon pinging against the sides of the cup. I went to hand it to her.

"Place it right there on the corner of the end table," she said.

I put it down where she'd requested and backed away. Almost instantly she took a sip. That was good. I looked for her reaction. There was none, no trace that she thought anything was wrong or different.

My mother took a big sip from her cup.

"Is this regular tea?" she asked.

I tried to hide my reaction. "It's the tea we usually use ... it's whatever was in the canister."

"It tastes a little bitter, that's all."

"Would you like another cube of sugar?" I asked, picking up the tongs.

"No, that's fine."

Jack reached for the pot to pour himself some tea.

"I'm sorry! Let me do it!" I exclaimed as I tried to brush aside his hand and take the pot.

"I think I can pour my own tea."

"Sure, of course, let me get the milk."

I poured milk into his cup as he poured the tea. I deliberately tipped in extra milk—the more milk, the less tea; the less tea, the less sleeping powder he'd drink.

"Hey, I'd like a little tea with my milk!" Jack snapped.

I stopped pouring. "Sorry."

"You've practically ruined it," he said.

"Do you want me to pour it out?" I offered, starting to get to my feet.

"Sit down," Liesl ordered.

"Sure." I settled back into the seat. "And you like lots of sugar." I picked up the tongs and then dropped three cubes in his cup.

"If I'd known that pointing a gun at you would make you less of a jerk I'd have got one myself a long time ago," Jack said.

He poured tea in the fourth cup—my cup.

"Only half a cup for me," I said. I poured the milk in immediately, added three cubes of sugar and stirred. I brought the cup up to my lips, pretended to take a sip and then returned the cup to the saucer on the table.

I tried to do a mental calculation about how this might work. Usually my mother added one spoonful of sleeping powder to a glass of milk. I'd probably dumped in the equivalent of six or seven or maybe eight spoonfuls. There were probably five cups of tea in the pot, so that meant this was at least a regular dose and probably closer to two.

I remembered from reading the package that larger people had to take a bigger dose. Jack was the biggest, my mother next, and Daphne was lighter than her by at least twenty-five pounds. That would mean that the same amount should affect her harder and faster. Her cup was more than half empty—but so was my mother's. Jack hadn't drunk much at all.

It usually took my mother about twenty minutes to get to sleep. Would a bigger dose work faster—or maybe it would keep you asleep twice as long? Either way, if all went well, Liesl and my mother and maybe Jack would be asleep soon. I wanted Liesl to be knocked out, but once that happened I wouldn't be able to get any information out of her. I had to act now. Maybe she'd let something slip that could help us.

"You're a very good spy," I said.

"As are you and your brother."

How strange! It was like we were complimenting each other on getting good grades at school.

"I never would have suspected you of anything," I said. "Juliette wasn't bad either. Have you two been friends for long?"

"I'd never met her before in my life until we were sent on assignment."

"Did you know Jack and I were once captured and almost forced onto a U-boat?"

"I wasn't told that."

"It was when we were involved with Camp 30. You must have had a terrible trip, by the way, when you crossed the ocean."

"It was very hot and smelly and—how did you know we came by U-boat?"

"That's the only thing that makes sense. I imagine that's how they'll evacuate you, too, when this is over."

She didn't answer, but I knew already from her reaction—it was like "he knows."

"That Case guy," I said, "I knew he was a suspicious character within thirty seconds. He really gave me the creeps. Guy looked like a rat."

She laughed. She'd now confirmed that she knew him, and pretty much suggested that he was another spy.

"My guess is that there are between ten and fifteen of you in the plant," I said.

She didn't answer.

"I guess you don't know," I said, tauntingly. "They probably wouldn't trust you with everything that's going on."

"I know everything. That doesn't mean I'm going to tell you everything."

"What difference is it going to make?" I asked. "It's not

like we're going anywhere, unless you want me to hold your gun for a while?"

She smiled. "Always a gentleman."

"So I guess you know why this isn't going to happen until midnight, right?" I asked.

"Well ... yes ... because it is late and dark and there's less chance of it being discovered."

"It would be later and darker at two in the morning, but midnight is when they can kill the most people."

She looked alarmed.

"Think about it. They're not only trying to destroy the plant, you know, they're trying to kill the people who work there, the people you've gotten to know and like, innocent men and women and—"

"Were they so innocent when they made the shell that killed my father?" she demanded, suddenly angry and loud.

"Your father?"

"It was one of those shells that killed him as he slept," she said bitterly. "Those 'innocent' women who stand on the line and joke and laugh and gossip, they are the ones who made that shell, and it is for my father that I am doing this."

There were tears in her eyes and her hand was shaking even more. I wasn't trying to get her riled up. I wanted her calm, restful, asleep. What could I say now?

"I understand," Jack said. "I understand completely. You're doing this for the same reason that George and I are ... for our family. I'm sorry about your father."

"Thank you," she said softly.

"He must have been a very good man," Jack said. "Because no matter how much you were pretending with me, I know that you are a nice girl ... I really did care for you."

"And I for you. I am so sorry it has come to this."

Jack lifted up the teapot, stood up slightly and filled her almost empty cup. That was strange. And then I noticed that his cup was almost untouched. He poured in milk for her and added the sugar cubes, stirring them in.

"You know, this war isn't going to last forever," Jack said.

She laughed a little. "And when it's over, I'll still be seven years older than you."

"But we could be friends. A toast to friendship."

Jack lifted up his cup, and Liesl smiled and did the same. They clinked their cups together, like a toast, and both brought them up to their mouths. I could see Liesl drinking and Jack pretending to drink. Jack knew something was happening, but how?

My mother must have thought that Jack was insane, or at least lovestruck. But I knew Jack wasn't crazy, and I didn't think he was lovestruck—at least, not any more.

Somehow he'd figured out that something was happening and he was playing along.

I noticed that the pistol was no longer pointed straight ahead; it was sagging toward the floor. Liesl was smiling, but there was a glazed look in her eyes. I glanced at my mother. She had a similar look, very peaceful, and she was smiling when there was no reason to smile.

Jack let out a big yawn. Almost instantly, both my mother and Liesl yawned as well. My mother's eyes were glazed over, and Liesl's chin started to fall toward her chest, her eyes were half closed. It was working, they were falling asleep!

Liesl's head jerked as she caught herself drifting off. She reached over and took another sip from her tea as if she was trying to use it to wake herself up.

"More tea?" Jack asked her.

"Please ... yes."

Her words were slightly slurred. I really hoped she hadn't noticed. We needed her to nod off without realizing it. Both her chin and the pistol started sagging toward the floor—more and more, until the gun was no longer aimed at us. Was this the time to act, or should we wait?

Jack got slowly to his feet. She didn't notice. He reached over and pushed the barrel of the gun down and away. Then he took it right out of her hand. She didn't react. She didn't respond. She was asleep, and Jack was holding the gun.

CHAPTER TWENTY

I POUNDED ON THE DOOR with my fist. I didn't see any lights. Maybe he was asleep … no, it was too early for that. Maybe he was out. I pounded harder. If he was asleep, I'd wake him up. I was making enough noise to wake the dead.

The door opened ever so slightly and a woman peeked out through the gap—a chain was holding the door in place so it couldn't open wider. Was I at the wrong house? It was snowing so heavily that I could hardly see the houses from the street, so maybe this wasn't Mr. McGregor's home.

"Yes?" the woman said, formally.

"I'm looking for Mr. McGregor, the principal. Is this his house, and is he in?"

"It most certainly is his house, and at this time of night in a storm like this where else would he be?" she demanded.

"I have to talk to him. It's important."

"I'm sure you think it is, but it will have to wait. You can talk to him at school."

"It can't wait that long! It's a matter of life and death!"

"George?" Mr. McGregor's face appeared now above the woman's. I felt a burst of emotion so strong that I thought I might cry out for joy.

The door closed and I could hear the chain rattling, and then it opened again. I was practically bowled over as Mr. McGregor reached out and grabbed me by the arm, pulling me in as a gust of wind pushed me forward. The door slammed shut instantly.

"I'm sorry, I had to talk to you and——" I stopped, stunned. In his right hand, pointing at the floor, was a pistol. I stared at it, and then up at him, in shock.

"When I heard the pounding on the door I thought this might be needed," he said. "Let me put it away."

"No!" I exclaimed. "Don't put it away, you might have been right. I've got to tell you what's happening at the——" I stopped when I remembered that the woman who'd answered the door was standing right there. Who was she? Was it okay to talk in front of her or what? She was older—like a grandmother——but that didn't mean anything.

"It's perfectly fine for you to speak in front of my wife," Mr. McGregor said. "She knows everything about everything."

"*Every* wife knows everything about everything," she said, "but this wife is a former agent of the Canadian government."

"That's where we met," Mr. McGregor said. "It was love at first sight the first time I saw her handle a sidearm."

"It took me a little longer to warm up to him," she said. "He was handsome, but a bit of a blighter, if you catch my drift."

They both laughed.

"But you didn't come to hear about our courtship," Mr. McGregor said. "Why are you here?"

"The plant is going to be attacked, destroyed, tonight!"

Both of them stopped laughing.

"And how would you know that?"

"Because we have a Nazi spy over at my house."

"You have *what*?"

"A spy, an agent. She took us prisoner with a pistol."

He looked worried and shocked.

"But it's okay. We captured her. Jack is watching her now. That's not important. They're planning on blowing up the plant tonight at midnight, and we have to tell Bill, and we didn't think it was safe to phone him or—"

"It wouldn't have done any good, I'm afraid," Mr. McGregor said. "The phone lines have been taken down by the storm ... or ..."

"Or the lines have been cut," his wife said, "in anticipation of the attack, in order to make sure that Camp X can't become involved in any attempt to prevent it."

"Exactly what I was thinking," Mr. McGregor confirmed.

"But we have to get word to Bill. Somebody has to go there and get him!"

Mr. McGregor looked at his watch. "It's almost nine. In this weather, along these roads, even if someone got there in time, it would be too late to send help."

"But we have to try!"

"We'll try, but we may have to take matters into our own hands. Come, I have to question your prisoner."

"You can't do that," I said.

"Why not?"

"We had to use sleeping powder. We put it in her tea and knocked her out."

"Brilliant!" he said. "But you and I will have to interrupt her beauty sleep."

I'd thought he was going to be angry, so that wasn't the response I'd expected.

"Elsie," he said to his wife, "you need to get dressed, take the car to Ralphie's house and send him in his truck straight away to Camp X."

"Who's Ralphie? Can he be trusted?" I asked.

"Trusted with our lives," Mr. McGregor said. "Tell them they need to come ASAP, that an attack is planned for midnight."

"And that the attack is from the inside," I said.

"Inside?"

"It's people who work at the plant. I think they're already there, and the explosives are already in place. I think it has to do with the steam plant and the service corridors that link it to all the buildings."

"Good. Tell them to coordinate their efforts at that location and—"

"And tell them they can't come in through the gates," I said. "Some of the Veteran Guard are enemy agents."

Now Mr. McGregor looked shocked. "That is a very serious concern. Do you have proof?"

"No proof, only what Liesl … the spy … what she said before she was knocked out. If I'm right, and some of the guards are in on it, then the whole place will go up at the first sign of any interference."

"Then that leaves only one way in," Mr. McGregor said. "They'll have to come in over the fence. At least the storm is perfect cover for that—that's one knife that cuts both ways." He turned back to his wife. "And as soon as Ralphie is dispatched, you come back to George's house. We'll need the car, and I'll leave you to guard the prisoner."

"And take care of our mother," I said. I felt a bit embarrassed to say the next part. "I sort of had to give her the sleeping powder, too."

"She'll be in good hands," Mrs. McGregor said. "I'm also a registered nurse."

Mr. McGregor took his coat from the hook behind the door. He slipped the pistol into the pocket as he pulled it on.

"Be careful," his wife said. She reached up and gave him a kiss on the cheek.

"*Bonne chance, mon chéri.*"

We stepped out and into the teeth of the storm. Each time out it seemed like it was worse than the time before. I ducked my head and pushed through the wind and the snow rising into drifts on the ground. Mr. McGregor was at my heels. It felt good to know that he was carrying a gun. It couldn't protect me from the storm, but there were worse things out tonight.

Back at our house, Liesl was still seated and asleep, but she was now tied into the chair with a bright yellow rope wrapped around her a half-dozen times. Jack stood over top of her, casually holding the gun. My mother was asleep, lying on the chesterfield, softly snoring, oblivious to everything that was happening around her.

"She's just a girl," Mr. McGregor said.

"And we're just a couple of kids," Jack said. "What's that got to do with it?"

"Good point." He bent down beside her. "What's her name?"

"Daphne, no, Liesl!" Jack said.

"Liesl, can you hear me?" Mr. McGregor said loudly into her ear.

She moved slightly, but her eyes remained closed.

"Liesl!" he yelled, and he slapped her across the face. I jumped in surprise—I hadn't expected that.

She came to, and her eyes opened slightly. She looked around, completely confused and dazed.

"Liesl!" he yelled. "The attack, when will it take place?"

Her eyes started to close and he slapped her again, her head jerking to one side with the impact.

"When is the attack!" he demanded.

She mumbled something that I couldn't hear or understand.

"Louder!" he yelled. "Speak louder!"

"Tonight," she said. "Tonight ... mid ... midnight."

Her eyes closed. He took her face in his hands and squeezed and they popped opened again. She looked scared, almost crazed. He put his face right down so he was staring into her eyes.

"Where will it be?" he demanded.

"The plant ... DIL."

"*Where* at the plant?"

"Every ... everywhere."

He released his grip on her face and her head slumped over onto her chest.

He stood up. "That's all the proof we need," he said. "That means that we have only one course of action." He paused. "The three of us need to go to the plant and stop the saboteurs."

CHAPTER TWENTY-ONE

"CAN YOU MOVE over a bit?" I asked.

"And where do you think I'm going to go?" Jack questioned. "This is a trunk, not a stateroom."

We were in the dark in the trunk of Mr. McGregor's car, and it seemed like he was hitting every bump between our house and the gatehouse. This was how we were going to get onto the grounds without anybody knowing it.

"Can you at least move your elbow so it isn't digging into my side?" I whispered to Jack.

"It's not my elbow," he hissed.

"Well, something's digging into me."

"Shut up and don't move, or you might get *shot* by accident."

I realized then what had been digging into me—the pistol that was in Jack's coat pocket, Liesl's gun. Mr. McGregor had shown Jack how to use it and handed it to him, saying that he "might need it." Jack knew about guns. Growing up on the farm, we'd both fired rifles before.

I tried to shift away a bit. The safety was on—I was sure. I didn't want to end things with me being shot in a car trunk.

"I'm coming up to the gate!" Mr. McGregor called out. "No more talking or noises!"

The car hit a bump and then slowed down, rocked and came to a stop.

"It's a fine evening!" Mr. McGregor sang out loudly.

"If you're a penguin or a polar bear," a voice—the guard's voice—answered.

"Can you believe my wife came out to the Community Hall to play bingo on a night like this?" Mr. McGregor said loudly.

"Women, weather and bingo are three forces of nature!" the guard replied. "And you'd be a fool to try to defy any of them."

Mr. McGregor laughed. "I'm almost tempted to make her walk home. I tried to call but the storm has knocked out my phone … it's dead!"

"All the phones in the whole facility are down," the guard said. "I'm thinking my relief may not come and I'll be stuck here for the night."

"I guess there are worse places to be stuck … like at my house if I made the wife walk home."

The guard laughed.

"You'd better get out of the storm, and I'd better be on my way," Mr. McGregor said.

I heard the gears grind and the car started moving. We were through the gate. So far so good.

I tried to picture our route in my mind. We had to curve around a number of buildings to come in behind the main plant and enter by the back stairs—the stairs that led to Mr. Granger's office. We had to hope that he'd still be there and that he'd know what to do. If not, it would be just the three of us.

We'd left Mrs. McGregor behind with our mother and Daphne ... Liesl ... both sleeping peacefully. Mrs. McGregor had arranged for help. They'd be moved from our house to a "safe house." That was in case another enemy agent came, but also because of the danger from the plant. If we weren't able to stop whatever was planned, it wasn't only the plant that was going to be destroyed but all the houses in all the streets around it— and all the people in those houses.

Mr. McGregor and his wife had talked briefly about trying to evacuate the area, but they'd quickly decided they couldn't do that without tipping off the enemy that we were on to them. Those people sleeping in their houses couldn't be warned. Their safety was dependent upon what we were doing, their safety and the safety of everyone in the plant. Hundreds, no, *thousands* of lives depended on what we were about to do. That was too overwhelming for me to think about.

The brakes whined, the car came to a stop and the sound of the engine died. I heard Mr. McGregor get out and slam the door closed. The trunk opened and light shone in. Mr. McGregor offered me a hand and I climbed out. Quickly I pulled up the hood of my coat so nobody could see my face and looked around. I couldn't see anybody. Between the thick snow and the darkness I couldn't see far or well—and neither could anybody else. Our enemy's advantage was going to be our advantage as well; the knife cutting both ways, like Mr. McGregor said.

What I did see was Mr. Granger's car tucked in beside the door. Why had I been so stupid? Why hadn't I insisted on seeing him?

Mr. McGregor slammed the trunk closed. "Lead the way," he said.

Hoods up, hiding our identity, we trudged through the snow. The door was open and we were soon in the stairwell, sheltered from the storm but also from unseen eyes. Jack started climbing the stairs and I was right on his tail. I felt a rush of adrenaline rising with each step. Mr. Granger would know what we should do and he'd have people he trusted who could help us do it. Jack opened the door from the stairwell leading to his outer office and we both skidded to a stop.

There, sitting at the desk, was Juliette! She looked as shocked and surprised as we felt, and for a second we all froze. She jumped to her feet and Jack rushed forward, throwing himself over her desk, knocking her down. I ran over as the two of them were on the floor, struggling and thrashing around and—she had a gun in her hand, and Jack was fighting to knock it loose!

I jumped forward, throwing my full weight right on her arm—she squealed in pain and the pistol dropped from her hand and skidded across the floor.

"Get the gun!" Jack shouted.

I scrambled over and grabbed the gun, and then I heard the door opening behind me—thank goodness Mr. Granger had heard us. But it wasn't Mr. Granger—it was a man, a stranger, and he was holding a gun! He brought the gun up and aimed it at me, and I heard the explosion of a bullet fired! I blinked ... as he crumpled to the ground.

I spun around, shocked, confused, unable to understand what had just happened. Mr. McGregor was standing in the doorway to the stairwell, his pistol in his hand, smoke rising from the barrel. Before I could even think to react, Jack scrambled to his feet and pulled out his pistol. Juliette remained on the floor, whimpering, rolling, holding her wrist, and for a split second I felt sorry for what I'd done. Then I remembered who she was and what she would have done to us if we hadn't tackled her. There was no time for sympathy.

Jack crouched down and edged his way to the door leading into Mr. Granger's office, holding the gun out in front of him. I aimed Juliette's gun at the door as well. Mr. McGregor came forward. He motioned for Jack to move aside.

"Hello!" yelled out a voice from the office. It was Mr. Granger! "Is somebody there?"

"It's us!" I called. "It's us!"

There was a hesitation. "George? Is that you?"

I went to answer and Mr. McGregor put a finger to his lips to silence me. I didn't understand why, but I wasn't going to argue with him. Slowly he moved to the doorway and then, gun first, leaned into the office. He turned around to face us.

"It's all right … it's clear."

Mr. Granger was in a chair in the corner, and Mr. McGregor was trying to untie the ropes that bound him.

"Bring the girl in!" Mr. McGregor yelled. "And drag the body in here as well!"

"Her first," Jack said, pointing at Juliette. "Get up," he ordered her.

She looked up. There were tears rolling down her face and she was obviously in pain, clutching her wrist.

"That wasn't a request," Jack said.

He grabbed her by her good hand and hauled her to her feet, and she let out a yelp of pain. He gave her a slight push that propelled her into the office.

"Sit over there," Mr. McGregor ordered, pointing to a chair in the corner, and she meekly sat down.

I turned back around to see Jack dragging the man in. If he wasn't dead, he was certainly unconscious. As the body moved, it left behind a dark-red stain on the concrete floor.

Mr. Granger was free and on his feet and he closed the door behind Jack.

"Thank goodness you came," Mr. Granger said. "I wish I could have put a bullet through that man's head myself."

It was then that I noticed that Mr. Granger's face was cut and bruised. It was obvious that he'd been beaten.

"How long have you been a captive?" Mr. McGregor asked.

"Three, maybe four hours. I have to assume that tonight is the night."

I nodded. In a quick burst we told him what we knew and what we suspected.

"Oh my God ... this is worse than I feared. We have to call in help from Camp X."

"The phone lines are dead," I said, "but somebody has been sent to alert them."

"A confidant of mine," Mr. McGregor said. "He'll get there and bring back help, but with this storm ..."

Mr. Granger looked at his watch. "We don't have much time. We'll have to deal with this internally. I'll alert my guards and—"

"You can't!" I exclaimed. "Some of the guards are part of the plot."

His eyes widened in shock. "Are you sure of this?"

"As sure as we can be," I said. "Besides, can you be completely sure that *none* of them are involved?"

He shook his head. "I can't guarantee that, but there are some who are above reproach, so I'll ask them to report to my office."

"I'm afraid that won't work either, old chap," Mr. McGregor said. "No orders can come from this office, or that will alert them that you're free."

"But if we can't rely on outside help and I can't use any of my guards, that means that there are only the two of us."

"Not two," Jack said. "Four ... four of us."

Mr. Granger looked at Jack and then at me, as if he was weighing up our strengths and weaknesses. "Right. You're right. There are *four* of us to stop this plot."

I felt a surge of pride—and fear—flow through my body. I was proud that he thought that he could count on me, and afraid that he simply had no choice, because we were all he had.

Mr. Granger walked up to Juliette. She was seated, hunched over, clutching her wrist and quietly sobbing.

"I'm sorry about your wrist. It must hurt badly," he said.

She nodded her head.

"We'll get you to a doctor as soon as possible, but first we need your help."

"I won't help you," she snarled through clenched teeth.

"If you don't help, you're dead."

She laughed. "I am a prisoner of war—you can't just kill me."

"I didn't say *I* was going to kill you," Mr. Granger said. "In less than two hours this plant will be destroyed and you will be killed with it, because you're going to be right here, tied up in this chair, counting the minutes until your death. Are you prepared to die for your cause?"

She didn't answer.

"It is in your interests that we stop this plot. If you help us, I can arrange for you to be helped, an arrangement offered."

"What sort of an arrangement?"

"I'll ask that they not shoot you as a spy," Mr. Granger said. "Instead you'll finish the war as a prisoner, and at the end of the war you will be released, as all prisoners are released."

Again she didn't answer.

"I have no time for this. Either you co-operate or we leave you here to die and we go on without you."

She remained silent.

"Fine!" Mr. Granger said. "Tie her up and let her die for her cause." He turned to walk away.

"Wait!" she exclaimed.

He turned back around.

"What do you need to know?"

CHAPTER TWENTY-TWO

MR. MCGREGOR MADE SURE the knots were tightly tied.

"Anything more you need to say before I put on the gag?" he asked Juliette.

"No, nothing," she said. "I've told you everything."

"Then maybe you should just wish us luck."

He slipped the gag over her mouth and tied it off so she couldn't yell for help. She'd said all that any of us wanted to hear——and it was worse than we'd imagined.

Juliette knew that at least fifteen buildings——the largest and the ones where the most explosive or flammable materials were stored——had been wired with plastic explosive. What she didn't know was exactly which buildings they were. Mr. Granger could make a pretty good guess at it, but even he couldn't be certain.

All of the explosives and all of the wiring were underground with the pipes in the service corridors. Those wires led back to the steam plant—when the explosion was triggered, the steam plant would be destroyed too, and anybody in there would be killed.

Juliette had confirmed the numbers—at least two guards, at least five women working on the lines, and she thought two men at the steam plant were part of the plot. All of them knew that the explosion was planned for exactly midnight, and they were to go on with their normal jobs until just before then. At that time they had to get clear of the plant, get away and meet at a pre-arranged spot on the edge of town. We already knew three agents who weren't going to make that meeting.

Mr. Granger picked up Juliette's gun, the one I'd taken from her, and checked it for bullets. It was fully loaded.

"George, this one is for you."

"Me?"

He handed it to me. "And I have to warn you—"

"Don't worry, I'll be careful."

"I know you will ... but that's not what I was going to say."

"You weren't?"

He shook his head. "George, if you need to, you have to use it. Do you think you could shoot somebody?"

I shook my head. "I don't know."

"That's an honest answer. But if Mr. McGregor had hesitated you'd be dead now."

"I guess you're right."

"I know I'm right. You have to remember what's happening here. If you aren't prepared to take a life—possibly an innocent life—you could put thousands of lives at risk here tonight, not to mention the hundreds of thousands of soldiers who would be put at risk if their source of ammunition was destroyed."

I gulped. I knew he was right. We now had less than two hours to get to those fifteen buildings and disconnect the wiring, while avoiding being seen by enemy agents. If we were seen, they might set off the explosives with us standing right beside them. I remembered something Bill had once told me about plastic explosives. He said that if a piece the size of your hand was detonated under a car, not only would the vehicle be completely destroyed but also the people in it would be vaporized—they wouldn't even be able to find *pieces* of the bodies.

I held the gun out in front of me and looked at it carefully. If I needed to, I could use it ... I hoped.

"Let's get going," Mr. Granger said.

We slipped into the big hooded coats that he had given us. Employees at the facility who had to work outside wore them; we'd look like everybody else innocently walking around, doing their jobs at the plant. More important, we wouldn't look like us. It was a little bit different with Mr. McGregor. Nobody knew who he was—at least as far as we knew—so if necessary he could walk into buildings, walk among the other workers and not tip them off.

We opened the door and the wind almost blew it off its hinges. The storm was still raging. If anything, it was stronger than before. I had to think that it was still our ally, working to offer us protection, hiding us from prying eyes. We travelled in a straight line with Mr. Granger leading. I followed behind, then Jack, and finally Mr. McGregor at the end. That was reassuring. I'd seen him in action and I was glad he was on our side.

The snow had settled deeply everywhere, but in places the winds had created drifts that were two to three feet high. I kept to the trail that Mr. Granger created. We circled around to the side of the main building. The evening shift was on, so there was light coming from the windows. As we passed by, hidden in the darkness, I was able to look inside and see the lines working at full speed, women and a few men working away, oblivious to us … to what was going on … to what might happen. And there was no way we could tell them. To warn them was to risk everything. If we tried to evacuate the people from the line, the enemy agents working inside would know we were on to them. All of those people in there were depending on us. They didn't know it, but their lives were in our hands.

"It's right around here," Mr. Granger said. "Somewhere under the snow."

He started stomping his feet as he moved around—then there was a metallic sound. He used his feet to clear away the snow and we all helped. I could see metal sheeting, and as we cleared it a handle became visible.

"Step back," Mr. Granger said.

He reached down and pulled, and the metal sheet came up, revealing the steam pipes and the service corridor. In the darkness I couldn't see the bottom, though I knew it was barely a couple of feet below. We all had flashlights but we couldn't risk using them.

"That looks awfully small," Jack said.

"It'll be a pretty tight fit," Mr. Granger said, "but I think I can fit around the pipes and—"

"It's not as tight a fit for me," I said.

Everybody turned to me.

"I can do it easier than anybody else … I can find the explosives like we discussed."

Somehow I was hoping that somebody would argue, but nobody did. Mr. Granger took my hand and helped me lower myself in. I had to squeeze by the two massive pipes, and I could feel the warmth from the steam they carried right through my coat. I knew the corridors weren't deep but I couldn't see the bottom and it was a little unnerving to lower myself down. I stretched out my leg …

"I'm touching the bottom … I'm okay," I said.

"We're going to set the door back down now," Mr. Granger said.

"What?" I gasped.

"That way you can turn on your flashlight without the light being visible."

"Yeah … okay … fine."

I wriggled by the pipes and spread myself out beneath them. It was a really small space, so small that I couldn't crawl on my hands and knees. I'd have to drag myself along on my stomach. Digging into my pocket, I pulled out the flashlight and rested my thumb against the switch. I wanted it ready. I looked up as the metal sheeting was lowered and the little light that was coming from above was extinguished, leaving me in complete darkness. I flicked on the flashlight and the whole tunnel became illuminated.

I was lying in a little tunnel, with concrete floor and walls. With the help of the flashlight I could see that the tunnel ran on, smooth and straight, for as far as I could see, both in front of me and behind me. Above were the two massive steam pipes. Now, with the outside storm muffled, I could hear them hissing and humming as the steam surged through them.

I ran the flashlight beam along the length of the pipes. If I'd been an enemy operative running wire to trigger an explosion, that was where I would have put it. I couldn't see anything, though. I reached up and ran my fingers between the two pipes and ... bingo! I pulled down two thick metal wires. I pulled harder and a length dropped down. It ran in both directions—toward the building that housed the main production line and also toward the steam plant. Was this the ignition wire? I had to be sure.

I dragged myself forward toward the building. With one hand on the flashlight and the other on the wire, pulling it down, I moved forward. But with each foot forward I moved farther from the safety of the door and the people above it and closer to the explosives. The storm became more muffled, and aside from the sound of the rushing steam, all I could hear were the noises I made dragging myself along and my own breathing.

Soon I began to hear other sounds, though—machinery and voices. For an instant I had a rush of fear—was somebody else in the corridor?—but then I realized I'd crawled so far that I was now underneath the building, and those were the voices of people working on the line. I continued to shuffle forward. It couldn't be much farther. It didn't need to be much farther. I was already under the building and—there it was.

The wires ended and were embedded in a clump of plastic explosive wedged between the pipes. It was at least twice as big as my fist, enough to blow up the entire building and the people in it. I pulled the wires out. Without an electrical impulse, it couldn't explode. This building was safe. One down, fourteen to go.

It was incredibly difficult to try to turn myself around. I rotated my shoulders and moved up, twisting my body around the pipes until I was able to spin around. I started to crawl away, and then stopped. The wires I found had been removed, but what if there were other wires, inserted from the other side? Or what if someone discovered that the wires had been removed? They could push them back in, or run more wires—I had to take the plastic explosive with me.

I shuffled backwards, aiming the flashlight up at the plastic explosive. I knew it wasn't dangerous any more … but still. I tried to remember everything I knew about plastic explosives. They were like mud. They could be pushed and prodded and actually moulded into a shape, like modelling clay. They needed an electric current running through them to detonate. Without that current, they could be thrown on the ground or stomped on or even have a bullet fired right through and they wouldn't go off. I had nothing to worry about. Nothing. I was sure. Positive. Almost positive.

Carefully I grabbed the clump—it was hot to the touch from the steam pipes. I pulled and it came off in one big chunk. There it was in my hand, enough explosive to destroy a building. I stuffed it in my pocket. I put the flashlight into my mouth so that I could see my way and have both hands free to move. I hurried along the corridor and almost overshot the trap door before I looked up and saw the three of them standing above me, the trap door partially open and snow flowing through the gap.

"I did it!" I practically yelled. "I got the wires!"

Squeezing past the pipes, I was grabbed by strong arms and pulled straight out of the hole and placed on the ground. The trap door was lowered quietly back into place.

"Where was the charge placed?" Mr. Granger asked.

"It was wedged between the pipes, right under the building."

"Plastic explosive?"

"Yes."

"How big was the charge?" he asked.

I reached into my pocket and pulled it out. "This much." I handed it to him.

"My goodness," Mr. Granger gasped. "I've never actually seen this much before. We're going to have to get to each of the wired buildings. If they're using charges this big, any one explosion could be enough to blow the whole plant up. But we don't have time!"

"We need to break up into two teams," Mr. McGregor said. "We can move twice as fast."

"There still won't be enough time."

"Then we'll have to move faster!" Mr. McGregor said.

"We can't move any faster without increasing our risk of detection. Besides, we still don't know for sure exactly which buildings are wired," Mr. Granger said.

"But we have to try! We can't just give up!" Jack exclaimed.

"We're not going to give up. We have only one choice. We have to find the place that the wires all lead to ... the place where the detonation will take place. It must be in the steam plant. If we can disarm that ... we'll deactivate them *all*."

CHAPTER TWENTY-THREE

"THERE'S A DOOR at the very back and another off to the side," Mr. Granger said. "Mr. McGregor will station himself at the back door, and Jack, you take the side entrance."

They both nodded.

"From here on in, nobody leaves. Anybody exiting those doors should be considered a threat. If they cannot be captured they are to be killed. Jack, do you understand?"

Jack nodded.

"Better to take one innocent life than to risk thousands. Good luck, men."

Jack and Mr. McGregor moved along the building toward their positions, and Mr. Granger and I moved along the side of the building in the other direction. Inside were stored thousands—no, *tens* of thousands—of shells. All loaded with explosives, waiting to be shipped out.

Mr. Granger had chosen this building specifically. It was close to the steam plant, but not too close. It had a limited number of people working inside, and it was probably one of the targeted buildings, which meant that there were explosives and wires leading out of it to the steam plant, to the spot in the steam plant where all the wires led, where the detonation would take place. Following those wires would lead to the spot where the wires came together, the point of detonation, and to the people who were going to do the dirty work.

I had to assume that we hadn't been seen, or at least that anybody who might have seen us had no idea that we posed a risk to the plot. As far as anyone could tell, we were a couple of maintenance men walking through the storm. Together, the four of us had already cleared the explosives from the four biggest, most important buildings. There wasn't time to do any more—it was already twenty minutes after eleven.

"You stay right behind me," Mr. Granger whispered over his shoulder.

There was no need to tell me again. I felt safer hidden behind him.

"The others should be in position by now," he said. "Are you ready?"

I nodded.

He pulled out his pistol. I reached into my pocket and

put a hand on my gun. It was reassuring and disturbing at the same time.

He opened the door and we stepped inside and almost bumped into a member of the Veteran Guard, with a rifle on his back.

"Hey, Mr. Granger, what are you doing here this time of—?"

"Put your hands up!" Mr. Granger was aiming his pistol at the guard to back up his demand. The man looked shocked and didn't move.

"Now!" Mr. Granger snapped.

The shocked look remained but he did as he was told. Still aiming his pistol at the guard, Mr. Granger leaned forward and took his rifle, handing it to me.

"I don't … I don't understand what you're doing, sir," the guard stammered.

"You're McDonald, correct?" Mr. Granger asked.

"Yes, sir, that I am, sir, but you must be mistaken if—"

"Silence!" he hissed. "You can put your hands down. How many people are working in this building tonight?"

"Including me, thirteen."

"Thirteen … you sound very certain of the number," Mr. Granger said.

"I am, sir. I was thinking that it was a real unlucky number, sort of like the Last Supper."

"McDonald, you have family who work here, don't you?"

"Two daughters and my wife, sir."

"And are they working tonight?" Mr. Granger asked.

"My wife's at home, sir, but both my girls are working the main line ... off at midnight, like me, and I'll be walking them home. I always arrange to work the same shift as my girls ... they're grown women with children of their own but they're still my girls, and I don't like them to be out alone at night."

"Very considerate. McDonald, has anybody been acting strangely this evening?"

"Strangely, sir?"

"Different, peculiar, anything out of the usual?"

"I don't know about strange, sir, but Johansen has been telling everybody that he's not feeling good. Said he had to leave early, really upset when the foreman wouldn't let him ... they finally agreed he could leave a bit before the end of shift."

Big surprise there—anybody who knew what was going to happen would sure as heck want to leave early.

"But he's still here?" Mr. Granger asked.

"Should be leaving soon," Mr. McDonald said.

"George, give this man his rifle back."

I hesitated for a split second before I realized why he had chosen to trust him—if his daughters were both here and working, he didn't know anything about the plot to blow up the plant. If he had, they would have been long gone and far away.

"Corporal McDonald," Mr. Granger began, "we are in the midst of a crisis. It is necessary for us to detain every person in this facility and hold them for questioning."

"Yes, sir."

"When we get farther in I want you to train your weapon on Johansen." He turned to me. "George, you are to do the same."

I nodded.

"If he doesn't comply immediately, if he tries to run, or digs into a pocket like he's searching for a weapon, he is to be shot."

"Shot?" Corporal McDonald questioned.

"Yes, shot. You will follow that order as if your life, and the lives of your two daughters, depend on it," Mr. Granger said. "Because, Corporal, they *do* depend on it. Where are the workers?"

"All inside the storage vault."

"Lead the way."

The Corporal opened up a sliding metal door that opened onto a large room where row after row, shelf after shelf were filled with shells and bombs. It was an incredible sight. Visible among the shells were seven or eight women and two men.

"That man, over there," Corporal McDonald said, pointing, "that's Johansen."

"George, you stay at the door. Remember, nobody passes."

Mr. Granger walked in, pistol at the ready, and the Corporal followed right behind. He walked up to the group of people that included Johansen. I didn't hear what he said, but I saw them all raise their hands into the air. They moved in my direction, with their hands still raised, the Corporal behind them, rifle at the ready.

"Up against the wall," Corporal McDonald said to them, "and keep your hands up where they can be seen."

People looked confused and scared. Johansen looked particularly scared. I would have been too, if I were him and knew what was going to happen.

Mr. Granger came toward us. He had three more people—two women and a man—also with their hands up.

I did a quick count. We had nine, and he was bringing three more, so that was thirteen including the Corporal. The last three joined the first group against the wall, hands in the air.

"Corporal, there are two men, one rather young and the other somewhat older, guarding the back and side doors from the outside. They are wearing coats similar to ours. Please inform them that the building has been secured and they are to come inside now."

"Yes, sir."

Mr. Granger turned his attention to the people standing in front of us. Some looked concerned, others angry, and two of the younger women seemed almost amused. Johansen was shifting from foot to foot and he appeared to be sweating.

"I'm sorry for having to treat you all like this," Mr. Granger began, "but we are in the middle of a difficult situation. I'm afraid you will have to be detained, here in this building, until we can complete our investigation. You should be freed by one or two in the morning at the latest."

There was a chorus of groans and complaints.

"I cannot wait that long!" Johansen protested.

Instantly I knew what Mr. Granger had done. Anybody who knew that the explosives would go off at twelve would now be desperate to leave.

"I'm afraid you have no choice," Mr. Granger said.

"But I am sick … very sick … I think it is my appendix … I need to see a doctor. Maybe you could come and question me there at the hospital."

A small smile came to Mr. Granger's face. "That won't be necessary. I'll do a medical examination right here."

He walked toward Johansen and placed the gun right against his temple. He ran his free hand under the man's jacket and—

"I think I found the source of the pain in your side."

He removed a pistol—it looked identical to the one I was holding, the one I'd taken from Juliette.

"That is for my protection," Johansen protested. "This is a dangerous place and I work into the evening and go home alone in the middle of the—"

"Shut your mouth or I'll shut it for you, you filthy spy!" Mr. Granger snapped. "I should put a bullet into your head right now and be done with it."

Johansen stopped talking. Judging by his expression, he was pretty sure that Mr. Granger would follow through with his threat. But Mr. Granger took the gun away from his temple and stepped back. Johansen wasn't the only one who was relieved.

Jack and Mr. McGregor appeared now, along with Corporal McDonald.

"Corporal McDonald, we have caught a spy. Your suspicions about Johansen were correct."

The Corporal looked pleased.

"Unfortunately, there may be more than one spy in this group. We don't have time to check and we can't risk being wrong. You must hold all of them here until you receive further notice."

"But we can't stay here!" Johansen protested. "We have to leave … the explosives will kill us all!"

"Explosives? What is he blathering about?" one of the women asked.

"There are explosives, here, under the building, and they are to go off at midnight and—"

"We will remove those explosives," Mr. Granger said, cutting him off. "You will be safe here."

"Are you going to remove *all* of the explosives from *all* of the buildings?" Johansen asked. He sounded panicked. "We must leave the facility … get off the grounds or we will die!" he screamed.

"One more word and you'll be dead *now*." Mr. Granger pushed the pistol against his temple one more time.

"Everyone, listen. We are going to remove the explosives from beneath this building. Once they are removed, you are safe. The walls of this structure are made of reinforced concrete and will protect you from any explosions. But there will be no explosions. We're going to stop them from happening."

Mr. Granger stepped back. "Corporal McDonald, you are in charge. If any of them attempts to escape you are ordered to shoot them. And if he even *speaks* again," he said, pointing at Johansen, "you are *ordered* to put a bullet between his eyes."

CHAPTER TWENTY-FOUR

JACK REACHED DOWN and pulled the wires out of the clump of explosive. Without an electrical impulse to detonate it, it was harmless. This building and the people in it were now safe. It was strange that the building that held the most explosives was the safest place to be. It was the people *leaving* the building who weren't so safe.

Jack went to climb down into the service corridor. I grabbed him by the arm.

"Let me go down first," I said.

He hesitated.

"I'm smaller, Jack."

"No question about that—you're downright puny."

I smiled. It was somehow reassuring to have Jack make fun of me.

"I can move faster. And if you go down first and get stuck, I won't be able to get past you," I explained.

He bowed from the waist. "By all means, ladies first."

"It takes one to know one," I snapped.

"Well at least I'm not—" He smiled. "We don't have time for this now, but later, I'm going to lay a beating on you."

"What did I do?"

"Nothing. Just for old times' sake."

"Well, as long as you have a good reason."

Both of us took off our coats. It was a tight fit, and the coats were only going to get in the way. Besides, we weren't going to need them. The rest of the way was going to be inside—inside the service corridor from this building to the steam plant. I reached into the pocket of my coat and removed the pistol and the wire cutters. I would need the wire cutters. I hoped I wouldn't need the gun.

I climbed through the trap door, squeezed past the pipes and dropped down to the bottom of the corridor. Jack squeezed through until he was lying down behind me. It felt good to know he was right there.

"It's now twenty minutes to twelve," Mr. Granger said from above. "You have fifteen minutes to get into position. Can you do it?"

"We can do it."

"I wish there were some way that either myself or Mr. McGregor could go with you."

"So do I," I admitted. "But that's not an option. We'll do our job."

"If anybody can, it's you two. By the time you get to the steam plant the building should be deserted."

"I wish we could be sure of that," I said.

"We're as sure as we can be. Would you blow up the building with yourself inside it?" Mr. Granger asked.

Of course he was right. They'd probably run the last set of wires out of the steam plant and somewhere into the field, so they could detonate the explosion from far enough away to have a chance of surviving it. The problem was, with all the snow, the wires would be hidden. The ringleaders would be somewhere outside, hidden by the snow, watching to make sure nobody came too close to the wires that ran across the field. By going through the service corridor, we'd stay invisible, and we could cut the wires from the inside.

"There's probably a five-minute window," Mr. Granger said, repeating what we'd already talked about.

The enemy agents we'd captured had all said the same thing—they were to leave the buildings by ten to twelve. That probably meant that the men who were going to detonate the charges would do the same. If we got into the steam plant right after they left, we'd be alone—we'd be able to disconnect the charges inside, find the wires leading out and cut them.

"We'll be covering you from outside the building," Mr. Granger said.

"Anybody tries to get in, they get a pill in the head," Mr. McGregor added.

"A pill?"

"A bullet," he said, touching a spot between his eyes.

Mr. Granger lowered the trap door, throwing us into darkness. I turned on my flashlight and the first hundred feet of the service corridor became brightly lit. Beyond that it was still hidden in darkness.

"Turn your flashlight off."

"What?"

"Turn off your flashlight. We'll use mine only and I'll aim it a bit in front of you and not so far down the tunnel. We don't want the light to warn anybody up ahead that we're coming."

"Oh, sure ... that makes sense."

I turned off my light, and for a split second we were thrown into complete darkness before Jack turned his on. I felt an instant rush of panic followed by a wave of relief.

"Start moving," Jack said.

The light spread out a dozen feet in front of me. I started moving, using my elbows to propel me, my body dragging behind. As Jack moved, the light bounced up and down, sometimes blocked by my body. I kept one hand on the wire, pulling it down as I pulled myself forward. The light and the wire were leading me to where I had to go. The hissing of the pipes above our heads was the only sound, and it muffled the noise of us moving along.

As we moved I tried to picture our passage. We had now left the ammunition storage building behind. We were outside, underground, with a few feet of ground and six inches of snow above us. Somewhere in front of us was the steam plant. How much farther it was and, more important, what awaited us there were both unknown.

We had a plan, but it wasn't really a complete plan. So much would depend on what we saw and found and how we'd react to it. And I guess as important was how the people there would react if they saw us ... we had to hope they'd already left before we got there. If not, well, we both had our pistols.

The path in front of me was almost all darkness. I stopped and looked back. Jack had fallen thirty feet behind. It wasn't as easy to travel while holding a flashlight. I could help speed him along. I turned on my flashlight and lit the way for him.

He shielded his eyes. He wasn't only holding the flashlight. In his other hand he already had his pistol out.

"Turn off your light!" I hissed.

He switched the flashlight to his other hand and turned it off. Now, with one hand free, he was able to move more easily, but not much more quickly. Jack was struggling to fit through the service corridor. It was a tight fit for me, but he had to squeeze his body between the narrow walls. He kept moving until he finally came in behind me.

"I can't move as fast as you," he puffed. "You know what this reminds me of?"

I knew exactly. "Being in the escape tunnel at Camp 30."

"Yeah."

"But this is smaller ... tighter," I said.

"Are you still having nightmares about the tunnel?"

"Not so much," I said. "I figure soon enough I'll start having nightmares about this, instead."

Jack laughed, and for a brief second I almost lost the seriousness of what we were doing, the danger we were in. It was just Jack and me, fooling around.

"At least here we don't have to worry about cave-ins, we're nobody's prisoner, and we have the guns," Jack said.

"We have *some* of the guns." I paused. "There are people with other guns who could be waiting for us at the end of this tunnel."

"Not if we time it right. We'll be alone in the building with time to do what we need to. What time do you have?"

I aimed the flashlight at my watch. "Fourteen minutes to midnight."

"We'd better hurry up and get to the end of the tunnel. You lead and I'll light the way again."

Jack put on his flashlight, and I turned off mine. I started forward, the wire between my fingers and the light showing the way. Part of me was caught up in the adrenaline rush. I wanted to get there, and get there as quickly as possible. But another part of me wanted to stop, turn off the flashlights and sit in the dark, out of sight and safe. Would these service corridors be safe? If there was an explosion in any of the buildings, wouldn't the flames shoot right through all of the tunnels? Maybe this was the *least* safe place in the whole complex!

I looked back again. Jack was again far behind. I stopped to wait.

"Keep moving!" Jack called out.

"You want me to go on without you?"

"I can't keep up. If you get ahead of my light, turn your flashlight on—but be careful. Don't let the beam go too far ahead. Don't let the light give us away. In case they haven't left yet. When you get to the end, wait for me before you climb out."

"You don't have to worry about that."

Even more than not wanting to go on, I didn't want to go on alone. But there was no choice. I started crawling. Very quickly the light from Jack's flashlight faded away until it was illuminating only the space between us, and not the path ahead of me. I flicked on my flashlight. I knew I had to keep going. I knew, with or without Jack, I had to do this.

I aimed the flashlight so that the beam of light was ahead of me, but not too far ahead. I kept focusing on that little trail of light and tried not to peer into the darkness or think about what was beyond it. I put my head down and kept moving. I shuffled forward, one hand holding the flashlight and trapping the strand of wire as I moved.

My elbow slammed against the side of the corridor. I tried to shift over a bit but the other wall was too close. I turned the flashlight on the wall—the cement blocks had shifted, collapsed inward, and the tunnel was much narrower. I had to get through. I rotated my shoulders and wiggled forward and stretched myself out. I was pressed on both sides but slipped through—only barely, though. I'd made it ... but could Jack?

I didn't have time to wait to ask. I had to keep going forward. He'd get through. He *had* to get through. I kept crawling.

The seconds turned into a minute and the minute into two and three and four and—the wire became stuck. I pulled it but it didn't come down ... wait ... maybe this was the spot.

I turned off my flashlight and I was in total darkness. No, not total darkness. There was a little streak of light coming from above. I followed the strand of wire with my fingers. It led up, between the pipes, and then disappeared through a metal trap door. I was now under the steam plant.

I looked back down the tunnel. I couldn't see a beam of light to mark where Jack was. He was somewhere back there, but how far? And more important, how long would it take him to get here?

I turned on the flashlight and looked at my watch. It was eight minutes to midnight. If it took him three minutes to get here we'd still have five minutes to find the charges, the bundle of wires, and cut them and—that was enough time. Besides, the longer I waited, the greater the chances of the building being empty. I still had time.

I tried to picture what was up above the trap door. I had a pretty good idea. In my mind I could see the corridor that ran around the perimeter of the steam plant right above my head. All along the corridor were trap doors that led into the service corridors that carried the steam pipes to all the other buildings. Coming out of this trap door—coming out of fifteen of the trap doors—were ignition wires. When Jack and I had cut each of those wires, all of the buildings would be safe. I had to cut the wires and get back into the service corridor and out of sight. Easy.

I turned the flashlight onto my watch again. I was relieved to see that it was still eight minutes to midnight

so I had ... it couldn't still be eight minutes ... at least a
minute had passed since the last time I'd looked. The
second hand of the watch was frozen in place! I tapped the
watch and it started to run again. But had it been stopped
for fifteen seconds or a minute or four minutes? I didn't
know, and I had no way of finding out.

I looked back down the tunnel. There wasn't a hint of
light. If Jack was coming, if he'd been able to get through
that narrow part, he still wasn't going to be here in time.
I had no choice. I had to go on without him.

I squeezed between the wall and the pipes until I was
pressed right against the metal grating of the trap door. If
I pushed it open, I could look out—I could climb out.
That thought sent a shiver up my spine that was in
contrast to the heat that was flowing through and around
me in the pipes.

Ear pressed against the metal, I listened. I couldn't hear
anything except the sound of the steam rushing through
the pipes. I *could* wait until Jack got here, but what good
would that do? If somebody was up there, I was dead. If I
waited, I was dead. If I tried and nobody was up there, I
could complete our mission. Only one hope. Besides, it
was better to die trying.

I pressed my hands against the metal and pushed. The
trap door started to rise—and groaned noisily. I wanted
to stop, but that was pointless. If there was somebody up

there I was already as good as dead. If nobody was there, then a little groan wouldn't matter. I pushed it open and climbed up on the pipes and looked through the opening. I was right, I had come out in the corridor that ran along the outer wall. I looked around. There was nobody. I was right inside the steam plant and I was alone.

I used all my strength to slowly lower the metal grating all the way until it swung down to the floor, landing open with a loud thud. I pulled myself up and climbed out and onto the floor.

Immediately I noticed that there were already three wires together on the floor, leading from—or to—something. They were probably coming out of other trap doors. I bent down, took out the wire cutters and snipped all three wires. Maybe they were coming from buildings where we'd already disconnected the explosive charges— maybe not. Either way, I couldn't take a chance.

I had to make a quick decision. This corridor circled the entire building. No matter which way I went I could, if I made a complete circuit, cut the wires individually. But, if I could get to the main door, all of the wires would lead there, and I could get them all at once. I didn't have time to stand here and decide, so I just moved quickly, cutting any wires that I saw.

I still held one strand of wire in my hand. I followed it as it led across the floor and then up the wall—right into a large clump of plastic explosive! There was a wire leading into it from the other direction ... and that wire ran through a second clump of explosive! This was exactly what Mr. Granger had said—they would have put charges here, too. I had to disarm the explosives and then follow the wires until they met.

I ran over to the first clump of explosive and ripped it off the wall, the wire coming free as I threw it to the ground. I ran toward the next charge. Any one of them was enough to destroy this building and kill me. If I didn't get them all, it would be like I didn't get any of them.

The second charge was also on the wall, but much higher up, above my reach. I had to find a ladder or something to stand on, or——I didn't have time for any of that. I backed up a few steps and then ran straight toward the wall, jumping into the air and smashing against it, clawing at the explosive. My fingertips hit against it and only half of the clump fell down, but the wires were dislodged, making the rest harmless.

Up ahead there was another trap door and a wire leading out of it. I took out the wire cutters, bent down and snipped it.

Instinctively I looked at my watch. It was running—five minutes to midnight—but that didn't mean anything. I had to hurry and——I stopped dead in my tracks. Lying there as I rounded the curve, blocking my way, was a body. I stood there, staring, trying to understand. The man was on his back, face up, unmoving and—wait, I recognized him! It was Frank, the man who'd shown me around the steam plant, and he was ... he was ... there was a dark stain on the floor, blood. There was no question.

There was also no question as to why he was dead. The men who worked here—the men not in on the plot, the men who weren't Nazi agents—would all have had to be killed. I could expect to find more bodies.

Carefully, quietly, I walked up, like I was afraid to disturb him. His eyes were blank, but open, and looking vacantly up at the ceiling. I stepped over him, trying not to touch the body, and Case appeared around the corner!

He looked as shocked to see me as I was to see him. Before I could react, he jumped forward, bowling me over. The wire cutters I was holding were knocked from my hands as we crashed to the concrete floor. I tried to scramble free, push him off, but he wrapped his hands around my neck, squeezing, strangling me. He wasn't big but his grip was like steel around my throat. I reached up and clawed at his eyes and he screamed in pain, and then he pulled my head up and banged it against the concrete floor! My hands fell limp as he continued to choke me. I didn't have the strength to break his grip.

My free hand pushed out and I felt the wire cutters. I grabbed them, and with the last bit of strength I had I swung them up until I heard them crack against his skull. He screamed in pain again, his grip loosened and I pushed him off! I scrambled to get away but he grabbed me by the leg. I spun around, the wire cutters still in my hand, and smashed him on the top of his head! Again his grip failed and I crawled away, desperately trying to breathe. His hands were gone from my throat but I couldn't draw a full breath, and—

He pulled out a pistol and aimed it at me. I thought about my gun, lodged down my waistband. If I could get it out—

"Get up!" he screamed as he got to his feet. There was blood pouring from his skull and his eyes were wild and red.

Before I could react, he reached down and grabbed me by the arm and hauled me to my feet. He pushed me forward.

"You stupid, stupid boy!" he yelled.

I stumbled forward as he pushed me again from behind.

"Now you will die."

There was something about the way he said those last words—quietly, with no anger. It was like a simple fact, and that scared me more than if he had screamed at me.

He kept pushing me along the corridor. We passed by other trap doors. Snaking through the cracks of some of them were wires, and those wires joined other wires. He was going to take me to the spot where all the wires led, where they joined and snaked out of the building. Once I was outside, Mr. Granger and Mr. McGregor would see me and Mr. McGregor would put a pill between his eyes and—

"Stop," he ordered.

I did what he said.

"Sit."

Without waiting he shoved me to the ground. It was then that I noticed that there were a dozen or more wires leading from both directions and they all came together right where he stood.

"You should not have come, boy. Now you are dead," he said.

"We're both dead if we don't get out of here."

He shook his head. "I was a dead man from the moment I agreed to this mission."

"We have to get out before the explosives are detonated!" I exclaimed. "It's almost midnight."

He looked at me. "How do you know midnight is to be the time?"

"I … I just thought that would be the time … when two shifts are here."

"You are a clever boy. Too clever, and that is why you will die."

"We don't have to die! Can't we leave the building? There's still time if we leave right now and—"

"There is time. No explosives will be set off until I set them off."

"You?"

"There is only me to do it."

I felt a wave of relief. If it was only him, then as soon as we stepped outside he'd be shot and the whole thing would be over before he could detonate anything.

I staggered to my feet.

"You sit down!" he yelled.

I stayed on my feet. "But we have to leave the building."

He shook his head. "We are not leaving."

"But if you set off the explosives then we'll both be killed!" I gasped.

"As I said, I was dead from the moment I accepted this mission."

Suddenly I knew what he meant. He'd never intended to get away. He was going to stay right here and detonate the explosives that would destroy the buildings—including this building—and take his own life.

"I thought I would be alone at the end," he said. "At least I have somebody to witness my triumph."

"It's a triumph to kill innocent men and women?" I snapped.

"In war there are no innocents. It is for my country that I do this, to ensure our ultimate victory."

"You won't be here to see it," I said.

"And neither will you. Now, sit and don't move or I will shoot you."

He pushed me over so that I fell backwards and into the wall, and something jammed into my back—the pistol. For a few seconds I'd forgotten about it, tucked into the back of my pants. All I had to do was pull it out.

I looked at Case. His head was still bleeding. Blood flowed over his face and stained his shirt. He was on one knee. He had placed his pistol on the ground beside him and he was focused on the wires. He was taking them, one by one, and threading them into what I assumed was the detonator.

"What are you doing?" I asked.

He looked up briefly but didn't answer.

"If I'm going to die, shouldn't I at least know how it's going to happen?" I asked. "It's not like I can stop you."

He nodded. "I am placing the wires into the detonator. Once they are placed I will be able to activate ... set off the explosives."

All I had to do was pull out the pistol and shoot him before he could do that—or before he could use his pistol to shoot me.

His attention was focused on the detonator. He was threading in the wires, one by one. I almost laughed when I thought that many of those wires led to nothing, had been cut or removed. Then I remembered that most of the others were still connected to deadly explosives.

Slowly I reached around behind my back. I felt the pistol and pulled it out by the barrel. I shifted it around so that I was holding it by the handle. I slipped my other hand back and clicked off the safety ... or had I clicked it on? I wasn't sure if I'd already had the safety on or not. I must have had it on. I couldn't look. Once I brought it forward I had to be ready to fire. I wouldn't have time to do anything else. I put my finger on the trigger, ready to fire the instant I pulled the gun out.

I kept my eyes on Case. He was still focused on the detonator, and his gun was on the floor. He hadn't noticed. I brought the gun forward and held it in front of me, but still he hadn't noticed. I glanced down at the safety. It was off. The gun was ready to fire. All I had to do was squeeze the trigger and it would be over—there was nothing he could do to stop me. I just had to pull the trigger and kill him ... kill him ... or ...

"Put your hands up!" I said, my voice cracking over the last word.

He looked up, and his expression was one of complete and utter shock. And then a small smile came to his lips. Why was he smiling?

"Do you have what it takes to kill a man in cold blood?" he asked.

I didn't answer.

"Well?"

"Yes, and I will if you don't put that detonator down *right now*."

He didn't.

"Some of the wires are already connected. If you shoot me, then I should still be able to push the detonator. Those buildings will blow up, killing hundreds, perhaps thousands. So, *you* should put *your* gun down or *I* will push the detonator."

"If I put down the gun, you'll connect the rest of the wires and then blow up all the buildings. So put it down and we'll all walk away alive."

"I told you, I'm already dead, whether I die here as a hero or in front of a firing squad as a spy. Either way I'm going to—"

I fired, and as the gun kicked back I saw the bullet rip into his chest. He staggered and stumbled and started to fall forward, dropping the detonator! I leaped up and grabbed for it as it tumbled toward the floor … it bounced off my outstretched hands and continued to fall, and I watched as it hit the floor and … and nothing.

I reached over and grabbed the detonator and held it in my hands. I stared at it. This small black box contained the spark to light a fire that could ignite the explosion to destroy the entire facility and kill thousands of people. And it was in my hands—small, weighing almost nothing.

It was over and——there was a loud noise, the sound of a door being smashed in. There was yelling and screaming from somewhere down the corridor. I could hear people running, and it was getting louder, they were coming this way!

I reached over and grabbed my pistol. Whoever it was, they were only getting to this detonator one way——over my dead body. I got up onto one knee and held the gun as steady as I could——my hand was shaking——and aimed it down the corridor, toward the voices and——it was Mr. Granger and Mr. McGregor and Bill and half a dozen soldiers! I lowered my pistol. It really *was* over.

CHAPTER TWENTY-FIVE

I SAT DOWN on the chesterfield beside my mother. She reached over and took my hand. I knew I was too old to have my mother hold my hand, but it felt good. It was something we both needed.

The last three days had been strange. Jack and I had been placed in the back of a van and driven straight here from the plant. I wasn't sure where "here" was. Between the dark and the storm, I hadn't seen much of anything through the van's small windows. I was told that we were in a "safe house." I liked the idea of being safe. We weren't allowed to go back to our old house. We hadn't been allowed to go outside.

When we'd arrived, our mother had already been here for a while, sleeping upstairs in one of the bedrooms. She'd slept for almost twenty-four hours before the medicine finally wore off. For all I knew, Daphne—or Liesl—

who had drunk more of the tea, might still be asleep. I could have asked Bill—he'd have told me—but I was almost afraid to find out. I knew what happened to spies. I didn't like Liesl, but I didn't want to think about her being shot. That image of Case was so fresh in my mind I didn't want to think of anybody else getting shot.

For three days we'd been debriefed. We'd been asked hundreds of questions about what had happened, we'd even written reports. And the same thing happened to Mr. Granger and Mr. McGregor. They were two of the very few people we'd seen since arriving here. It was like we were prisoners ... well, not prisoners, but we definitely had guards all around the building, inside and out.

Jack walked into the room. He sat down on the other side of our mother and she took his hand as well. Somehow that was as reassuring as her taking my hand.

My brother had been remarkably quiet. Partly it was because he was overwhelmed—we were all overwhelmed—by what had happened. Jack had emerged from the service corridor in time to see the action. He'd been wedged in, trapped, in the spot that had almost stopped me. His clothes had been ripped and torn and he had been cut and scraped as he'd desperately clawed his way through. I knew he felt bad about not being there for me, but it wasn't like he hadn't tried.

I also knew that he was still troubled about Liesl. He

must have felt stupid for letting her trick him like that, but he also would have been hurt. Jack had never had a girlfriend before, and to think that she really didn't care for him, that it was just a game ... well, that would have hurt a lot more than any cuts or bruises.

I looked at my watch. It was still ticking away. Bill was scheduled to arrive shortly, and then, we'd been told, we would discover our fate. I was certain we were going to have to move, change schools and change towns and maybe change names again. I didn't care. They could call me anything they wanted short of Georgina and I'd be happy to be gone. As long as we stayed anywhere near Ajax or Whitby I'd never be able to walk down the street without looking over my shoulder. I'd be waiting for something to happen or somebody to come after us. We were now a bigger target than ever. Not only had we stopped the Nazis from destroying the munitions factory, I'd actually killed a Nazi agent.

I'd replayed that scene in my head a hundred times over the past few days. I knew that I'd had no choice. I'd asked him to put down the detonator, and if I hadn't shot him he'd have taken me and thousands of other people to the grave with him when he destroyed the plant.

Bill had discovered that seventeen buildings had been wired with explosives. We'd managed to cut the wires to six of them, but if Case had pushed that button, if he'd been able to activate those charges ... I didn't even want to think about it.

I wondered if I'd ever be able to get those final images out of my mind. Him standing there, holding the detonator, and me firing the gun. It was like it was happening in slow motion. That look of shock on his face as the bullet slammed into him and—a knock on the door startled me from my thoughts.

"I'll get it," Jack said.

"No," my mother said, refusing to let go of his hand. "Come in!" she called out instead.

The door opened and Bill entered—followed by Little Bill. We shook hands and Bill gave my mother a big hug. Soon they were seated right across from us, and they started to make polite small talk with my mother. I'd waited long enough—I needed to know.

"Well, what's to become of us?" I asked, cutting them off.

Bill laughed, and Little Bill gave me a knowing smile.

"You certainly know how to cut to the chase," Little Bill said. He pulled something from the inner pocket of his coat. It was a newspaper. "Let me be the first to formally offer my condolences to your mother on the loss of her sons," he said.

"What?" I gasped.

He handed me a copy of the local newspaper, the *Whitby Reporter*. The headline read "Four Young People Killed In Car Crash." It detailed how Jack, Liesl, Juliette and I had been killed in an accident. Apparently, the driver, Liesl, had lost control of the vehicle and it had crashed into some trees.

"A similar story will appear in *The Commando*," Bill said. "Mr. Granger informed me that the editor, Mr. Chalmers, was very upset when he was told of your death."

Well, one thing was clear enough: We would never return to Whitby or Ajax or anywhere around here again.

"Mr. McGregor also told me that there were quite a few tears shed for you at school when it was announced," Bill said. "Apparently, a couple of the lasses fancied you, George."

I felt myself blush.

"Reportedly Mr. McGregor gave quite the eulogy at the school assembly. But yours was, of course, not the only tragedy," Bill said. "*The Commando* also ran an article about an accident at the steam plant that took the lives of five men, including Case, two other agents and the two innocent men they killed, one of whom had a daughter who attends the school." He paused. "Of course, the article says nothing about what really happened, only that five men were killed in an unfortunate industrial accident at the steam plant."

"Of course," I said.

"It is important that people in the plant and in the community never know how critical the situation became," Bill said.

"Or that their lives were saved by the actions of a very few people, including a fifteen-year-old and a twelve-year-old," Little Bill said.

"I didn't do anything," Jack said. "It was all George."

"This victory was due to the actions of four *men*, working together as a team, and I am proud to be sitting here across from two of those men. Your actions saved the lives of those people and the production of the entire plant. Without that production, without that ammunition, the course of the war might have turned against us," Little Bill said. "You boys are heroes."

He stood up and offered us both his hand and we shook it. I found myself blushing again.

"I am truly sorry that no one can know of your heroism. I'm sorry, too, that we needed to kill you in the story."

"Couldn't we have just moved away?" my mother asked.

"We wanted to make sure," Little Bill explained, "that you are no longer seen as a target by any enemy agents who might remain in the community."

"Oh, my goodness," she gasped. "I hadn't thought about that. And this will make us safe?"

"That is part of the plan for your future."

"But why should they believe the newspapers?" I asked, before I'd thought through how this question would worry my mother more.

"You're right, George, they would probably question the story, think that it was an article we planted," Little Bill said.

"So ... why put it in?"

"To back up the information that they received from their own agent."

Now I was confused.

Little Bill smiled. "We had help from that girl ... you called her Daphne."

"I'd like to call her some other things!" Jack snapped.

"Then perhaps one of them should be 'friend,'" Little Bill said.

Jack snorted. "She was an enemy agent, she took us prisoner, she was going to kill us!"

"I don't believe she actually could have pulled the trigger," Little Bill said. "She was an enemy agent, doing what she believed for her own cause and her own country, as were the two of you. But in the end she made a decision to safeguard your lives."

"I don't understand," Jack said.

"She agreed to make a phone call to another enemy agent, her contact. She informed him that she was on the verge of being captured, but that in her last assignment, to take your family prisoner, she had been forced to shoot you both."

"She was very convincing," Bill said. "I supervised her while she made the phone call. If I hadn't known the truth, I would have sent flowers to your mother. That girl was an *excellent* liar—probably the result of being a diplomat's daughter."

"So, the enemy will believe the newspaper story to be a cover-up, but they will also believe you to truly be dead. We assume that there will be no effort to find you," Little Bill said.

"But why did she agree to do that?" I asked.

"I think, in part, because she came to realize that perhaps her cause was not just or right," Little Bill said. "But more than that, I think she did it because she genuinely cares for Jack."

Jack looked surprised, shocked, but pleased.

"She suggested the idea. She also gave away the name and location of the agent she contacted," Little Bill said. "Once he's had time to pass on her message to others, we'll have him arrested. Her only motivation to do any of this was to provide for your safety. Perhaps to make up for what she did."

"And what will happen to her?" Jack asked.

"She'll be held as a prisoner of war, in isolation, with no contact with anybody except the other young lady."

"Juliette?" I asked.

"That's what you knew her as," Bill said.

"And they will remain in custody until after the war ends," Bill said.

"And then?" Jack asked.

"And then they will be returned to their families in Germany," Little Bill said. "But enough about them. You must want to know where you are going to be relocated to so that you can, to all intents and purposes, remain dead."

"I guess it has to be pretty far away," I said.

"I wonder if placing you boys on the moon would keep you out of trouble," Bill said.

"You're not going quite that far," Little Bill said. "We've decided you're going to spend the remainder of this war safely away from here ... far away."

"How far?" I asked.

"I am afraid it is necessary for it to be *very* far," Little Bill said. "But be assured it will be someplace where your entire past will remain unknown."

"So ... where are we going?" Jack asked.

Little Bill slowly shook his head. "The exact location is still being discussed. There are certain, shall we say, loose ends that need to be secured."

"When will you know?" my mother said.

"Within days, and you will be there within a week of that decision being made."

"Good. I need these boys to get settled in, get back to school. They've missed enough already," my mother said.

"I'm so pleased that you all understand the need for our plan," Little Bill said.

My mother's expression suddenly changed and she looked serious. "I was wondering how we're going to explain all of this to my husband. What should I say in my letter? I can't tell him any of what really happened, can I?"

"Not a word," Little Bill said. "But in any event, I don't think there will be time for you to write any more letters."

What did that mean? Why didn't we have time to write him any more letters?

"You'll have to tell him when you see him in person," Little Bill said.

"But that could be years!" my mother cried.

"Not so long as all that, I would imagine." He turned to Bill. "His plane is scheduled to land in Toronto within the hour."

"Whose plane?" I asked.

"Your father's," Little Bill said.

I couldn't believe my ears!

"But he might be a bit cranky," Bill said. "I doubt he's slept for more than a few hours over the past two days. That flight across the Atlantic Ocean on its own is long and difficult, but he first had to fly in from Africa."

"Africa ..." I could hardly believe he was saying what I thought he was saying. Was this really happening?

"My husband ... the boys' father ..."

"Will be touching down at the Toronto airport in the next hour," Little Bill said. "He will be accompanying you to your new location. That's where you will *all* live out the war ... together ... as a family."

My mother burst into tears. I burst into tears. Jack burst into tears.

"How can we ever thank you?" my mother gasped as she once again hugged him.

"No, madam, that is where you are wrong," he said. "The question is, how can *we* ever thank *you*? Your family has done more, risked more, than any one family could ever be asked."

My mother threw an arm around me and another around Jack and we hugged and laughed and cried. Our father was coming home! We were all going to be together!

"I must look a mess!" my mother exclaimed. "Do I have a few minutes to change and put on some makeup? And I don't know what I can do with my hair! Please, excuse me." My mother rushed from the room.

I should have been just plain happy, grateful, but there was something that was still troubling me.

"My father won't know anything about what's been going on, will he?" I asked.

"I am so sorry, boys," Little Bill said, "but until at least the end of the war, and probably beyond that, your actions must remain secret. Even secret from your father."

"But won't he have questions about why he was sent home?" Jack asked.

"An appropriate cover story has been arranged. And your father will be able to continue to make a contribution to the war effort, but in a different way. We will discuss that further in the car ride to the airport," Bill said.

"As long as we're all together, nothing else matters!" Jack exclaimed.

"Well," I said, "there is one more thing." I paused. "I know that after today we probably won't see either of you again ... ever."

"'Ever' is a long time," Little Bill said. "But I suspect that you are correct, at least until the war is over."

"But that's it," I said. "I remember something you said to me once, about when you were serving in World War I and they tried to send you home. You said the war wasn't over so it wasn't over for you." I paused. "The war isn't over ... for any of us."

Little Bill smiled and placed a hand on my shoulder. "I believe that your service to your country is now at an end. But if you are ever needed again, I have no doubt ..." He let the sentence trail off.

"If you need us again," I said, "you'll know where to find us."

Jack nodded his head in agreement.

"And we'll be ready!"

"I know you will," Little Bill said. "I know you will."